THE ROCKING OF THE OCEAN

THE SEQUEL TO BEACH ROSE PATH

BARBARA MATTESON

5 PRINCE PUBLISHING

Published by 5 PRINCE PUBLISHING & BOOKS, LLC

PO Box 865, Arvada, CO 80001

www.5PrinceBooks.com

ISBN digital: 978-1-63112-403-7

ISBN print: 978-1-63112-404-4

Cover Credit: Marianne Nowicki

F042125

For Savannah, my own Little Lovey.

Acknowledgments

I am incredibly grateful to 5 Prince Publishing for the extraordinary chance to publish my third book. Bernadette Soehner, you are my editing saint, and I am eternally grateful for all your comments in editing The Rocking of the Ocean. I am sure you wanted to pull your hair out at times, and because of all of your brilliant editing suggestions, The Rocking of the Ocean transformed into an exceptional book. I am now acutely aware of my use of exclamation points!!! (I could not resist!)

Also by Barbara Matteson

The Perfect Mrs. Claus

Beach Rose Path

The Rocking of the Ocean

THE ROCKING OF THE OCEAN

CHAPTER 1

OCTOBER BREEZE

Charlotte Templeton stood on the driftwood porch of her home as a light breeze blew in from the ocean, bringing with it the slight chill of autumn that tousled her wavy hair. The sunset was breathtaking, transforming the sky from a watermelon hue to a mesmerizing amethyst. Beautiful streaks of pink, lavender, and coral lit up the sky as the fiery red sun dipped below the horizon, casting a glow over the pearly gray ocean. Charlotte turned up the brown corduroy collar of her navy-blue barn jacket as the October breeze felt cooler than it did a few short weeks ago when, according to the calendar, it was still summer. And what a summer it was. It was her first Lobster Claw summer on Beach Rose Path. Life had taken Charlotte to the most unexpected places, where she formed fortuitous friendships and experienced the most unanticipated surprises, including a new romance. As swiftly as the summer months flew, she transitioned from her former role as a retail manager at a women's golf pro shop to the proud owner of her own store, The Shop at Beach Rose Path. Charlotte was also a homeowner of a charming bungalow conveniently attached to the shop.

"Lovey, not too close," Charlotte called as her yellow Labrador mix dodged the frothy white caps of the waves pounding on the beach. Lovey looked up before bounding toward her mistress, full of energy and kicking up sand with her enormous paws. Charlotte bent down to hug her panting best friend. Incredibly, another dog entered Charlotte's life—a dog she would love as much as her first, something she never imagined.

"Oh, you silly girl," she said as Lovey rolled on her back, kicking her legs in pure happiness, her head lolling back and forth with an enormous grin on her face. "Okay, sweetie, let's get you some dinner."

At that, Lovely flipped and stood obediently in military fashion, and the two of them headed inside the bungalow.

Charlotte poured kibble into Lovey's bowl, took a carrot from her kitchen counter, and placed it next to the bowl on the floor.

"Go ahead, it's dinnertime!" she sang as Lovey, with the gusto of a hungry teenaged boy, dug into her dinner, saving her carrot for dessert.

While Lovey chomped her dinner, Charlotte crossed the threshold that brought her from her cozy bungalow into her shop. She closed the shop early in the fall as the days became shorter and the tourists dwindled. It was still busy during the peak hours because the foliage in this part of Northern Maine was spectacular; however, as darkness descended earlier with each passing October day, the tourists retreated to their bed-and-breakfasts or hotels, allowing Charlotte to enjoy the quiet of the autumn evenings.

Although it was only six o'clock, she could already see a difference in the shortening of the days. She needed to turn the lights on earlier, but that was fine with her. Her first summer in Lobster Claw had been nothing short of magical, almost too good to be true, but then Charlotte had to remind herself that the success of The Shop at Beach Rose Path was because of her own blood, sweat, and tears—and there were many of those!—which she poured into the business; *her* business.

Charlotte arrived in Lobster Claw in May with a wounded

soul, having lost her job, her home, and her mentor. But through sheer determination to survive and to succeed, she successfully built herself a new world in a new place.

She gazed around the transformed storefront, once dusty and empty, and now filled with sturdy, cubby-style oak shelves displaying a myriad of T-shirts and sweatshirts adorned with the bold red lobster emblem of Lobster Claw, Maine. Tote bags hung on wooden pegs advertising The Shop at Beach Rose Path, with its now signature pink blossom beach rose atop a green stem with glossy emerald leaves. Charlotte also kept stocked the best-selling kitschy key chains with large red plastic lobsters proclaiming LC, ME. There were shelves full of books on the history of Northern Maine that were especially popular with tourists, as well as books by her favorite New England authors, including Louisa May Alcott and Nathaniel Hawthorne. Children's books about the local legends of the sea, especially the mermaids of Lobster Claw Bay, spilled from the bookshelves.

In the charming little seaside shop, the coffee table was covered in current magazines, creating a welcoming space for visitors to relax, read, and enjoy coffee and cookies. Her shop was quaint and homey, and customers agreed, as many returned each morning. After a leisurely walk on the beach, tourists would retreat to her shop for a cup of coffee and a look at the local paper. (Charlotte loved that Lobster Claw still printed their paper.) Then they would be off again, happily caffeinated before starting their days of sightseeing, whale watching, or taking a ferry ride to Camden courtesy of Callum's Pride Boat Tours, run by her dashing knight in shining armor, Duncan Kirk. Duncan. He was a gift given to her by the forces that brought Charlotte to Maine. She realized when she began her journey this spring, her life wouldn't be the same—that was impossible. Charlotte wasn't sure if she would be able to remain, or even wanted to, after the summer. But after she resurrected Rory Ruskin's little seashell shop and turned a handsome profit, Hamish Falconer, her father figure and mentor, had given her the keys to Beach Rose Path. Now she was the lawful and very happy owner.

Charlotte shook her head of silvering brown waves. Her hair now touched her shoulders, as she hadn't had a chance to cut it all summer, but she preferred it a bit on the wilder side—just like the terrain of her new home. She adored the way the summer night air blew tiny specks of sea salt upon it, making it even more untamed, more natural.

The loud munching of Lovey enjoying her carrot always made Charlotte laugh, and she continued to watch the sun sink into the ocean. She loved this time of the evening, the sunset hour, and spending it with Duncan, but he was in Boston for the day and would be returning later.

He had promised his former architectural partners at Grayson Dane Kirk he would consult on a project. Duncan was another lost soul who fled from Boston back to the security of his childhood home after a terrible betrayal. After reassessing the values and priorities in his own life, he lived not only his dream, but his father's, and launched what promised to be a successful ferry service, which kept him busy for the summer. With summer nearly over, Duncan was busy fulfilling his promise to his former business partners in Boston. Wrapping up the Boston Seaside Center renovation was on the top of his list, and once that was done, he planned to focus on growing his business in Lobster Claw.

A cool waft of sea air brought Charlotte back to earlier that morning, the warmth of his arms wrapped around her, the soft velvety feel of his well-loved leather bomber jacket, the smell of old leather mixed with his piney aftershave, and the downy softness of his day-old beard. The memory of his kiss goodbye remained vivid in her mind. His slightly chapped lips had pressed lovingly upon hers, and she could still feel their slight roughness. His sincere words echoed in her mind.

"I'll miss you," he'd whispered before he left, tightening his arms about her body. She could have stayed like that forever, but she'd eased away, smiling at his heartfelt words.

"Me too," she'd said, her hands caressing his sunburnt cheeks. She ran her fingers through his thick hair and leaned up to kiss him again. "You'll be home before you know it," she said, burying her head into his broad and strong shoulders. Goosebumps rose on her arms as the coolness of the sterling silver charm bracelet slid down her wrist, a gift from Duncan to commemorate their summer together.

"Home," he murmured. The stubble of his unshaven chin grazed the top of her head as he hugged her tighter. "We are home, aren't we?"

She gently pulled away from his embrace and was met with his smile that always melted her heart.

Charlotte laughed. "That we are, but if you want to come back, that means you have to go, and now, before traffic gets heavy." As much as she hated the idea of him leaving, she admired his dedication to William Grayson and Alfred Dane. She, too, was just as devoted to Hamish Falconer, her own guiding light.

Duncan sighed, his bomber jacketed arms loosened, and the warmth and comfort of his loving caress evaporated.

"Are you ever wrong, my dear Charlotte?" he laughed, kissing the top of her head.

"Um, no. Not when it concerns you and how much you detest a good traffic jam. Out you go," she said, smiling, her hands making a shooing motion.

"Ouch!" Duncan dramatically put both hands on his chest and pretended to fall. "An arrow to my heart. How could you?"

They both laughed as he embraced her once more.

"I'll text you when I get there," he said as the two of them walked from Charlotte's warm home out into the cool early morning air. Her old fleece jacket was not enough to break the cold sea breeze, but she didn't care—she wanted every second she could have with Duncan before he left.

Duncan took her into his arms and held her close. They each curved into the other, their lips meeting in a passionate kiss. The kiss imprinted on her mind—the chill of the air, the subtle dryness of his lips on hers, and the scent of his piney and spicy aftershave drifted in the cool air. As their kiss ended, Charlotte kept her eyes closed, capturing the feel of his lips and the scent of his cologne, comforting reminders of his presence that would have to last her until his return.

"Drive safely," she whispered as Duncan got into the driver's seat. He closed the door and rolled down the window, reaching for her hands and bringing them to his lips.

"I will," he said, releasing her hands. He turned the key in the ignition, bringing the motor to a roar.

"And," he said, "I love you." Those were words Charlotte thought she would never hear from another man's voice. Her heart quickened every time he said it, knowing she would never tire of hearing him say those precious and cherished words.

"I love you," she murmured, blowing him a kiss as he headed toward Sand Dollar Drive to the highway that took him away from her.

Now, twelve hours later, Charlotte conjured in her mind the feel of Duncan's arms hugging her.

"He'll be back soon," she whispered as she picked up Lovey's bowl to wash with the rest of her dishes. But for this moment, she wanted to bask in the love that she discovered with Duncan Kirk on Beach Rose Path. The dishes would wait.

CHAPTER 2

NEWPORT, RHODE ISLAND

"We cannot thank you enough for your help, Duncan," William Dane, one-third of the partners of the Dane Grayson Kirk Architectural Firm, said, opening the blinds of their thirty-fourth floor conference room in Boston's financial district.

"We knew there was something missing with this project, and we also knew you would know what that was," Alfred Grayson chimed in.

The sun that streamed in from the floor-to-ceiling panes of glass nearly blinded Duncan as he took a seat. He adjusted the chair so that his back faced the window. "You two conspirators want me back in the office," he said, laughing.

The cousins had designed and built many developments, such as the current Boston Seaside Center, as well other developments along the East Coast. Duncan suspected they most likely didn't need his help.

"Well, you know us too well," William said with a laugh. A man well into his seventies, he had never lost his enthusiasm for architecture and new projects.

"There is a prospect we'd like you to consider," Alfred said in a more serious tone. The younger of the cousins, he, like William, still maintained a child's excitement in creating beautiful urban outdoor spaces.

"We'll just cut to the chase. We've missed you," William said.

The words were spoken so earnestly and fatherly that Duncan could feel the affection pour from the elder gentleman as he laid his knobby hands on the table.

"Now, we know you have your life in Maine, which we appreciate and understand, along with your life with Charlotte. But we truly miss your *younger* input."

Duncan laughed, thinking that one thing he would not consider himself was young. "Pretty much everything I learned was from the two of you. What are you thinking about?"

William cleared his throat, a habit of his before he would make a proposition. "We're expecting something to come our way before year's end and we'd like for you to consult on it."

"Of course," Duncan said.

"We will email you all the details as soon as we get them ourselves, and we promise to do as much as we can via videoconference, but there might be the chance you'd have to travel, if that's okay with you. The job is scheduled for Newport, Rhode Island."

"That should be fine," Duncan said. "But if I can do as much over the winter as possible, that would be a bonus. I've got a boat business to run, you know," he said with a smile.

"Don't you worry, son," William said, rising out of his chair and moving toward Duncan, who also stood. "We know you have other priorities in your life, and who could blame you? We will keep our interference to a minimum."

"You know I'll never refuse you," Duncan said.

Alfred turned toward a mahogany credenza upon which sat a giant-screen monitor. He opened a drawer, pulled out a large manilla envelope, and handed it to Duncan.

"This arrived in yesterday's mail. Funny enough, the postmark is Newport, too. A good omen, I suspect."

Duncan looked at the envelope. The return address was from

S. Reese, Esq. Duncan shook his head in bewilderment. "Thanks. I don't know anyone in Newport. I'll look at it later."

"Perhaps someone else is looking for your expertise," William said, winking at Duncan as he patted him on the back with his wrinkled hand.

"My loyalty lies only with you two," he said, laughing, walking toward the office door "Talk soon."

"Safe travels, my boy," Alfred said.

Duncan headed toward the elevator with the envelope tucked under his arm. Once outside, he jogged to his pickup truck, having one more stop to make before heading back to Maine. "That can wait," he said, tossing the envelope on the passenger seat. He didn't give the envelope or its contents another thought as he pulled into the afternoon traffic.

CHAPTER 3

AN ENGAGEMENT

"Unbelievable," Duncan muttered as he sat in gridlock. His trip across Boston should have taken only twenty minutes, but a fender bender on Federal Street severely delayed him.

He took a deep breath, thinking that in a few hours, he'd be out of this mess and home to Lobster Claw and to Charlotte.

He checked his phone, as it was very apparent from the sea of cars and the loud horn beeping that he wouldn't be going anywhere for a bit. He texted Charlotte to let her know he'd be late, and to not wait up for him. Instantaneously, he received a text that brought a huge smile to his face.

I'll wait all night. Drive safe.

I will, my love, he texted back.

A tow truck was trying to weave its way through the dense traffic, but not one car budged. It was impossible for Duncan to move as well, so he decided to sit and enjoy the show. He laughed watching the truck wiggle like a caterpillar into what seemed like a massive parking lot. He glanced out the passenger window when the envelope caught his eye, making him scowl in annoyance. He disliked dealing with the mountains of paperwork generated by projects, but it was a necessary part of his job. He picked it up and scrutinized it more this time.

"Interesting," he murmured, ripping open the top of the envelope. The loud blare of a horn jarred him. He looked up and saw the traffic had parted like the Red Sea.

"Thank you, Lord," Duncan said, once again flinging the envelope back into the passenger seat as he stepped on the gas.

Fifteen minutes later, Duncan parked his truck in front of David Charles Jewelers. He hopped out of the truck and walked into the store, feeling a rush of cold air blasting from the air conditioner.

"Duncan!" David Charles, the proprietor, said. "I didn't expect to see you so soon. Such a pleasure."

Duncan reached out his hand to his old friend in greeting and shook it heartily. "Me, either, but I had something I wanted to discuss with you."

"Is it the bracelet? Is everything okay?" David asked nervously.

Duncan chuckled at David's unnecessary worry. "No, the bracelet is perfect. Charlotte loves it and never takes it off. And that's why I'm here."

"Is there another charm you'd like to add?" David asked, his hands already opening the immaculate glass case laden with the most exquisite watches, necklaces, and earrings.

"Eventually, but not right now. What I want to talk to you about is a ring."

"Oh, a ring?" David said, a cheerful smile unfurling across his face. "An engagement ring, I might presume?"

Duncan's face lit up with a smile. The cold air suddenly turned warm, as a flush of abrupt shyness overtook his senses. A surge of love flowed through his body at the thought of an engagement ring for Charlotte, and he knew he wanted to spend the rest of his life with her. He found comfort and warmth in her presence. She was a guiding light through his darkest hours. He was fifty-four and never married, and if he was going to marry someone, it would only be Charlotte.

Duncan inhaled and felt his body temperature return to normal. "I suppose you could say it's an engagement ring, but I have something very untraditional in mind. Do you have some time to discuss?" He knew exactly what he wanted, and if there was anyone who could deliver, it would be David.

"All the time in the world for you," David said, escorting him to a desk and chairs in a corner of the store. "Let me just get my assistant to cover the counter and we can chat. Take a seat. I'll be right back."

Duncan sat down and waited for David to return. He pulled his phone from his jeans pocket and saw a call had come in with a 401 area code. "Those two have me reined in already." He laughed, thinking that Alfred and William let the Rhode Island contractors know he agreed to consult. And he would, but on a very limited basis.

The tourist season had slowed after a very successful summer of ferrying vacationers up and down the Northern Maine coast. Charlotte had been incredibly busy with her shop. Things would pick up for her again as the fall tourists were coming in, and he wanted to help her. He also promised Tatiana Dulka, owner of The Blue Hydrangea art gallery, to help her with inventory. Duncan was going to be busier than he thought, but he promised himself he would never turn down anything that the cousins asked of him. He was indebted to them for his successful twenty-five-year career.

However, Duncan had entered another chapter of his life, one that didn't include the glamorous parties of Boston, but instead included quiet walks on the beach with Charlotte and Lovey. And he would not want it any other way.

Duncan wanted to propose to Charlotte, but he didn't know when he would pop the question. He did know the moment had to be special, and because of that, he wanted to be prepared with a ring like no other.

As he waited for David to return, Duncan's phone pinged. He took it from the back pocket of his jeans and saw a text from Ivy. It was a photo of her feet propped up on one of her exam tables. *Taking your advice!* she had texted, and he laughed, putting his phone back in his jeans pocket, recalling their conversation from earlier in the week.

"You'll know, big brother," his sister Ivy had said when he told her of his plans to buy Charlotte a ring. "Just make sure you get that ring ASAP, and carry it with you, because when that proposal moment strikes, you want to be ready."

"Yes, Doctor," he had said with a laugh. "Now take my advice and get off your feet—I want you in tiptop shape when my new niece or nephew decides to arrive." Duncan never expected that he'd be excited about the prospect of a baby entering his life, but he eagerly awaited Ivy and Andy's baby due in late May.

"All set," David said as he returned to the desk. "Now, what do you have in mind?"

The two men put their heads together as Duncan described, in great detail, what he wanted designed for Charlotte. David's fingers grasped colored pencils, and his hand flew across a sketch pad, carefully etching what Duncan described.

"How's this?" David asked, presenting his illustration to Duncan. He took the pad from David, amazed at how he perfectly captured Duncan's vision of the perfect ring for Charlotte.

Duncan shook his head in astonishment. "This is beyond what I imagined in my head. I didn't think I could describe it the way I saw it in my mind, but, but . . ." He was so overwhelmed by David's sketch, words escaped him.

"You did a great job describing it. It's obviously something very special to you, and for an extraordinarily special woman as well. Should we go with this? I can always—" David continued to study the drawing, his hand grasping the pencils.

"No," Duncan interrupted. "You can't improve on perfection. This is exactly what I wanted. Exactly."

"Wonderful," David said, putting down his pencils. "I should have this ready by Thanksgiving, if that works for you?"

"Thanksgiving?" Duncan asked in awe. "I was thinking more after the New Year."

"Not for you. I'll start working on it first thing in the morning, and I'll text you photos. Sound good?"

Once again, David Charles had earned Duncan's gratitude. He had done such a wonderful job on Charlotte's charm bracelet, there would be no one else he would ask to help design this special ring.

Duncan rose from his chair and extended his hand in friendship and gratitude. "I owe you big time for this," he said, shaking the hand of his old friend.

"Nonsense. Just an invitation to the wedding," David said.

Duncan left the jeweler feeling like the luckiest man in the world. His heart teemed with happiness at the anticipation of knowing he would soon be back home, not only in Lobster Claw, but in the arms of the woman who changed his life.

CHAPTER 4

TATIANA

The loud chime of Charlotte's phone startled her. She was fully engaged in surveying merchandise for the store, lost in online catalogs. She ordered a few items for the Christmas season, and heeded Tatiana's warning about the busyness around the holidays. Snow Cap Mountain, one of New England's premier ski resorts, was just ten miles north of Lobster Claw and produced a lot of tourist traffic. She shook off thoughts of beach towels, key chains, and the other sundry types of souvenirs and reached for her phone.

Traffic is heavy. Be home around ten. I hope that's not too late.

Charlotte smiled at the text. Even years later, the memory of the car accident that claimed the lives of her fiancé and beloved dog caused an intense feeling of anxiety whenever Duncan traveled the long distance between Lobster Claw and Boston.

Thanks for letting me know. It's never too late for you, she texted.

"His truck is like a military vehicle," she said with a laugh, convincing herself that he was safe behind the wheel. Even Lovey's pleading brown eyes seemed to tell her to stop worrying. "Oh, you're right. But you know how I am, Lovey. I worry about everything." She returned to her online catalogs. "Now, back to the fun stuff." She smiled as photos of colorful T-shirts, tote bags, and sun hats appeared on her computer screen.

Another ping suddenly expelled from her phone. "Oh, goodness!" Charlotte said, again reaching for her phone and reading the text.

Open your door, please!

"Tatiana," Charlotte exclaimed, as she closed her laptop and hurried to the front door. Lovey beat her there, her tail wagging furiously with anticipation. "Who's here, Lovey?" Charlotte said excitedly.

She swung the door open to see Tatiana Dulka standing on her doorstep, her arms laden with gifts.

"Tatiana!" Charlotte happily wrapped her arms around her friend.

Tatiana's long pewter hair blew like the silk of angels' wings in the evening air. The sapphire blue tartan shawl wrapped around her shoulders made her hair seem extra snowy, and her blue eyes glowed as if lit up from inside.

"What are you doing here?" Charlotte asked, surprised to see the woman who was not only her friend, but her confidant. She had only met Tatiana in May, but they had quickly become close friends when Charlotte moved to Lobster Claw. The older woman had taken Charlotte under her wing and helped to guide her into her new life in Maine. Their bond deepened when she discovered Tatiana was the long-lost love of Hamish Falconer, Charlotte's mentor, father figure, and former boss.

"Well, it's good to see you too," Tatiana said with a laugh, balancing the gifts in her arms, trying not to drop the packages on the door stoop.

"Let me help you with those," Charlotte said as Tatiana handed her two of the bags.

Lovey nosed Tatiana joyously, jumping tiny jumps and emitting high-pitched cries of happiness. She was just as excited to see Tatiana as Charlotte was.

"Oh, sweetie," Tatiana said, laughing and bending to greet the happy dog. "I'm only just back, but I will bake your favorite treats for you tomorrow. I promise," she said as the dog eagerly kissed Tatiana's face.

"Lovey, here's your store-bought treat." Charlotte chuckled, taking a rawhide from the package of treats she had ordered online. She dropped the goodie on Lovey's dog bed.

Lovey obediently pulled herself away from Tatiana, curled up on her bed, and crunched on her treat.

"That will keep her busy for a while," Charlotte said as the two women sat on the couch. "You look incredible. But I didn't expect you until next week."

"Oh, Charlotte, I cannot even tell you how beautiful Scotland is. I came back a bit earlier because Haleigh's parents were visiting from London, and I didn't want to be in the way. Of course they all protested, but I also didn't want to overstay my welcome, and I had to get back to the gallery to get ready for those leaf peepers— have there been many?"

"Not too many yet, but never mind them. Tell me everything. I'm just about to make a pot of chai tea. Duncan's on his way back from Boston and won't be here until about ten, so we have hours to talk."

"Oh, tea would be wonderful, thank you," Tatiana said, setting down the bags on the coffee table and shrugging off the tartan shawl. "But before anything else, I want you to open your gifts." Each bag was a different hue of plaid, tied with matching bows.

"The red bag is for Duncan, so we can put that aside, but this green one is for you, and the amber one for Lovey," Tatiana said, nodding towards the bags.

"Oh, you shouldn't have," Charlotte said as love surged within her for Tatiana's kindness and thoughtfulness. "This was your time with Hamish. You shouldn't be thinking of us."

"Nonsense," Tatiana said as her soft and warm hands clasped about Charlotte's. "If it were not for you, Hamish and I would never have reconnected." Charlotte felt her friend's grasp tighten as she spoke about the rekindled love she had found with Hamish.

"I never forgot Hamish, and I never stopped loving him and Annabelle," she said, mentioning the daughter they had shared. "I also never thought I would ever in my life see him again, but because of you, well, here we are, and he truly is my Hamish once again."

Whenever Tatiana spoke of Hamish, her blue eyes sparkled like jewels, and a faint pink blush rose upon her porcelain cheeks. Charlotte couldn't help but wonder if this was how Tatiana looked all those years ago when she first met Hamish—the pure and incandescent look of love shining upon her face. Charlotte still could not believe Tatiana and Hamish were romantically involved, albeit briefly, many decades ago, and that Tatiana had given birth to their daughter, who Hamish and his wife Hannah adopted. Until this past summer, Charlotte never knew about Annabelle, and all the events that led up to Hamish adopting the child. Nor about the child's tragic death.

Charlotte embraced her friend. The most precious of life's gifts, love, had discovered Charlotte and Tatiana again, and tears pricked Charlotte's eyes as emotion overwhelmed her.

"No more tears," commanded Tatiana. "Open your gifts."

Charlotte nodded, wiping the last of her tears away, and carefully pulled the artfully tied green satin ribbon. She reached into the bag and cleared away a mound of white tissue paper.

"Oh, Tatiana." Charlotte pulled out a luxurious green-and-black tartan shawl from the bag. She had never felt something as soft as the shawl, and the colors were vibrant and beautiful. "This isn't cashmere, is it?" Charlotte slyly asked, standing and wrapping the ultra-soft shawl around her shoulders.

"Oh, I knew that color would complement you with your pretty brown eyes and hair." Tatiana smiled.

Charlotte was touched by her friend's thoughtfulness. "It's

absolutely stunning. I don't know what to say. This must have cost—"

"You never mind that. I've passed up so many things in life because of a price tag and was full of regret afterwards. Money comes back. It's special, as you are to me, and you deserve a little luxury in your life. You work so hard," Tatiana said admiringly, as Charlotte adjusted the shawl over her shoulders. "It suits you beautifully."

"I won't take it off all winter. Thank you." Charlotte snuggled into the soft cashmere.

"You're very welcome. It's the least I could do."

"And how is Hamish?" Charlotte couldn't wait any longer to ask. Although she received frequent texts from Tatiana and Hamish, she wanted all the details that a simple text message could not relay.

"Hamish," Tatiana softly said. She sunk deeper into the soft cushions of the couch. "It was almost as if no time had passed at all. We haven't stopped talking for a moment, catching up on our lives. When he invited me to Scotland, I will admit I was hesitant at first, but now I feel it's become my second home."

The soft sigh of Tatiana's whisper emanated unmistakable warmth and gentleness. Charlotte heard the affection and tenderness radiate from Tatiana's words as she spoke of her love for the Scot—the same man who brought so much love and comfort to Charlotte during her darkest days after the deaths of Landon and Peppercorn.

"Hamish certainly is a special person," Charlotte said, heading into the kitchen for the tea tray. While she waited for the water to boil, she arranged the cups and saucers on the tray. Charlotte looked at Tatiana and noticed the far-away expression on her face. *She's still in Scotland with him,* Charlotte thought. She placed tea bags into the cups then filled the teapot with the boiled water. Returning with the tray, she poured water over the fragrant tea bags. She handed Tatiana her cup and saucer.

"I know you were concerned about Colin, but from what I gathered from your texts and emails, that was something you didn't need to worry about. Colin is a wonderful boy, well, man now," Charlotte said with a laugh, as she really only knew him as a child. When he turned eighteen, he left for college and then Scotland, and she hadn't seen him since then. However, Hamish always kept her updated on his son's family's activities.

"He told Colin everything that happened between us," Tatiana began, sipping her tea. "Hamish was so nervous. Colin always knew about his older sister, but not her true parentage. Hamish said when he found out he got up and hugged his father and said, 'Dad, you're a good man, a better father, and an amazing grandfather.' Which, of course, brought the old stalwart Hamish to tears. And he and Haleigh couldn't have been nicer to me."

Charlotte smiled, sitting down next to Tatiana. "Colin and Hamish were always so close. It devastated him when Colin said he was going to stay in Scotland after graduate school. But Hamish knew that he would eventually return to Scotland himself. What do you plan to do?"

Tatiana put down her cup into the saucer. "Right now we, we are taking things one day at a time. My home is here in Lobster Claw, my business, my wonderful friend," she said, reaching over to take Charlotte's hand. "It would be hard to leave, and Hamish knows this. So for now, we plan on splitting our time between here and Scotland. It might not be the best plan, but we're going to give it a go. Hamish will come back at the end of the month, and then it's our plan to return for Christmas. I'll stay until late winter and then head back here for the season."

"It sounds like the perfect plan to me," Charlotte said, tightening her own grip on Tatiana's hands.

"Now, enough of me," Tatiana declared. "More presents, and then I want to hear about you and Duncan. I know I've only been gone a month, but we have a lot to catch up on," she said with a wink, settling in for a nice long catch up with her friend.

"Well for that," Charlotte said, standing up and taking the teapot into the kitchen, "we are going to need plenty more tea."

"I also brought some pure Scottish shortbread," she said, pulling a tin from her tote bag, which she had laid on the floor. "You make more tea and I'll get out the cookies. Oh, Charlotte, look at us. Did you ever think in a million years that life would turn out like this? You and Duncan and me and Hamish? Finding love again? I most certainly did not."

"Before you arrived, I was thinking the same thing," Charlotte said, refilling the teapot with hot water. She put the top on the teapot and returned to the couch. "I was outside watching the waves roll in, and Lovey playing in them. If someone told me six months ago that my life would be this, a new store, a new job, a new dog, a new love in my life, I would have called in the men in the white coats. I still have to pinch myself every now and again to make sure this is real. But it is real. Lovey is real. The shop is real. Duncan is real, and so are you and everyone down at the Beach Block. I find myself so overwhelmed with gratitude, with love, I just . . ." Those blasted tears once again returned to Charlotte's eyes, but they were not tears of sorrow—they were tears of gratefulness and thankfulness. Charlotte's heart was so full of thanksgiving and appreciation, she could only express it through tears of joy.

"Oh, sweetheart." Tatiana leaned over the couch and wiped Charlotte's tears.

Charlotte was so touched by her motherly comfort and love.

"If there's anyone who understands how you feel, it's me. I am overwhelmed myself and cannot believe my good fortune, especially at this stage in my life. But we deserve to be happy," Tatiana said. "We've both suffered such heartbreak, heartache, and unimaginable losses. I believe this makes everything good that is happening in our lives even more special. We have endured our tragedies and now it is time for our happiness."

"You're so right. I know it's silly of me to cry."

"Never silly," Tatiana said. "You wear your heart on your sleeve, and that is so admirable. Never change that. Promise?"

Charlotte looked into Tatiana's eyes, feeling as if she could see her friend's soul. They shined with love, with hope, with friendship and loyalty.

"I promise," Charlotte said, wiping the last of her tears. "I'm suddenly starving. Let's dig into those cookies." She laughed as the two happily caught up on their lives for the last month on opposite sides of the Atlantic Ocean.

CHAPTER 5

THAT STORMY NIGHT

The green digital numbers on Duncan's dashboard clock glowed nine forty-five. "Right on time," he said, smiling as he made the turn onto Sand Dollar Drive. "Even a bit early." He slightly sped up toward the end of the dark road to Beach Rose Path.

Passing Elsie's Everything, Lobster Claw's general store and diner extraordinaire, called to mind that stormy night in May when he stopped in the store, seriously contemplating returning to Boston when he had noticed Charlotte. From the distressed look on her face, to the almost childlike way she followed Elsie around the store, to her bright brown inquisitive eyes and wavy chestnut hair that flowed down her neck, Duncan knew he wanted to be part of whatever quest she was on. That was the night he paid for everything in her basket when she realized she didn't have her wallet.

There was a woman, alone, out in the middle of a wild Maine spring nor'easter. Duncan knew there was something special about a person who would be crazy enough to be out in such a storm. And was he ever right.

As the victim of many poor decisions in his life, for which he only had himself to blame, Duncan was more than cognizant that he made one very right decision, which was staying in Lobster Claw. From the moment he laid eyes on Charlotte, he knew he wanted to know her. When Charlotte left Elsie's, he went right back home—his childhood, no-electricity home, which he retreated to after an emotionally fraught breakup with his former fiancée. At first, Duncan missed Boston and all its excitement, but as he settled into life in Lobster Claw with Charlotte, Boston could be as far away as the moon.

He knew Charlotte was determined to make Lobster Claw her home, and he realized his home was with her. He worked hard over the summer with Callum's Pride, making ferry runs up and down the northern Maine coast, ushering everything from tourists to sundry deliveries. Although he'd discovered there was a need for this type of service, whether it would be successful or not, only time would tell. Duncan now planned an expansion for next spring—to continue with the ferry runs and the idea that he concocted with Charlotte of a sightseeing business.

As Charlotte's bungalow appeared, anticipation made his heartbeat quicken. The glow of yellow light streaming through the windows was so inviting, and knowing Charlotte, his own little miracle, was waiting for him on the other side of the door filled him with pure joy.

He put the car in park in front of her house, and reached into the backseat for the box of chocolates he had purchased at Bridget's Chocolate Box with all of Charlotte's favorites. The big manilla envelope then caught his eye. Still assuming it was architecturally related, he grimaced at the thought of opening it. A potential design project, outside of what Alfred and William had discussed, was the last thing Duncan wanted to think about right now.

"There'll be time enough for that tomorrow," he said, getting out of his truck as the thought of sinking into the arms of the woman he loved propelled him to Charlotte's front door.

CHAPTER 6

ALONE FOR TOO LONG

Hamish Falconer sat in his well-loved and well-worn black leather chair in his study at his home in the Scottish Highlands. He had arranged his cup and saucer, his beloved cinnamon scones, and a steaming pot of chai tea. Inspired by Tatiana's love of the "nectar of the gods and goddesses," he sweetened it with a small dollop of thick golden honey. At first, the thought of infecting his straight chai with something so sweet repulsed him. He was loath to admit that he actually liked it, and now, whenever he poured a touch of honey—*just a drop!*—into his afternoon tea, his thoughts drifted back to Tatiana and their rekindled love.

Tatiana had been gone only a day, but Hamish felt her absence everywhere in his home, especially now, during afternoon tea, as he sat in solitude. The tea didn't taste as sweet, even with the honey, without Tatiana on the other side of the desk. Nor did the scones taste as fluffy and buttery and cinnamony—they tasted bitter, hard, and flavorless.

"Oh, who am I kidding?" Hamish scolded himself, throwing the half-eaten scone onto the saucer. He was miserable, and it was because Tatiana was not with him. Hamish deeply loved Colin, Haleigh, and Lachlan, and he couldn't imagine life without them, but the companionship of Tatiana made his life complete. It was a sheer miracle they found each other after all these years, and he did not want a second more to go by without the woman he loved. He had been alone for too long.

Hamish had no interest in dating, even years later when Colin was on his own and a married man. Over the years, Tatiana never left his mind or his heart, but he kept her in the past, never daring to contact her. His life was full as manager at Castle Loch Golf and Country Club outside of Boston, and the only woman who occupied his life after his wife's death was Charlotte, who he grew to love like his own daughter. Hamish remained close with her, offering his support, after her fiancé died. Then, last spring, the announcement came that Castle Loch would be under new management, and all employees received their pink slips—including Charlotte and Hamish. He wanted to decide when he retired, but the new management had done it for him. He had always planned to return to Scotland when the time came, but it arrived quicker than he expected. As Hamish planned his return to Scotland, he needed to ensure Charlotte's well-being and organized for her to stay at the property he owned in Lobster Claw, a property he kept as a secret as it was a special connection to a former life.

Unbeknownst to Hamish, his solitary bachelor days would end when he discovered that Charlotte befriended Tatiana Dulka in Lobster Claw. He knew it was time to see Tatiana and finally bring their past to a close. But the chapter did not close. Instead, another unexpected and beautiful one opened as Tatiana and Hamish resurrected their love that truly never died, and now Hamish did not want to waste a minute without her.

He looked out of his den window at the craggy Scottish landscape. It was beautiful in a rugged sort of way. The vibrancy of the autumn colors of a few weeks ago had now been muted, but still maintained their beauty. Russet and dark gold leaves blanketed the rocky hills, leaving the towering oaks with bare branches. He watched as the chubby squirrels, their mouths full of those leaves, darted among the branches—like a highway in the sky, with exits and detours, all leading to their winter nests. The bright red berries of the rowan trees, planted by his grandfather to ward off the evil hexes allegedly cast by country witches, attracted the attention of the neighborhood blackbirds. A flurry of snow had fallen, gently coating the leaves and the bare branches of the trees, making the landscape out of his window look as mystical as the ancient legends.

"Oh, Tati would love this," he whispered, watching the large flakes slowly fall from the gray sky and carpet the surrounding hills. Tati's beauty remained unchanged over the past fifty years and continued to enchant Hamish. He realized that the spell she had cast on him when he first arrived in the United States continued to hold true. His body still trembled, and his heart skipped a beat at the sight or the thought of her. She was just as lovely now, maybe even more so, with her long, thick platinum hair and blue eyes that sparkled like the sea. Her movements were as lissome as they were all those decades ago, and she still maintained her love for the fine arts, as evidenced by her successful little art gallery. It was The Blue Hydrangea that took her back to Lobster Claw that autumn, and although he absolutely understood that she needed to return, he regretted not going with her.

"Hamish," she had said last night before she boarded her flight for Boston, "before you know it, we will be together again. The weeks will fly. You'll see." Tatiana's petal-soft lips lovingly touched upon Hamish's. "Besides, you have that absolutely irresistible grandson of yours to keep you busy. Plus, I need to get home so I can spend all my money on buying that beautiful baby mountains of Christmas presents. And maybe one or two for you as well." Tatiana's beaming smile brightened Hamish's darkening soul, as the thought of not seeing her for several weeks crushed his already breaking heart. Hamish had embraced her one last time, drinking in the fragrant scent of lavender and the sea in her hair, on her clothes—the calming fragrance that never left her even after all these years. Tatiana blew Hamish a kiss and boarded the plane that would take her back home.

Home. "Where is home now?" he said aloud, looking out his window. The snowfall had ceased, and the dark of the pink and purple sunset lined the horizon of the hills. "Home is with you, Tati," he whispered as he planned how he could be with her. At home.

CHAPTER 7

SWEET CHILD

Exhaustion flooded Tatiana upon her return home from Charlotte's. It was a long journey from Hamish's Scotland home back to Maine. She had slept on the all-night transatlantic flight, and when she landed, she was rested and ready for the train ride to Brunswick from Boston, and then the drive in a rental car back to Lobster Claw.

After dropping off her rental, she hopped in a short taxi ride home, threw in a few loads of laundry, showered and went to pay Charlotte and Lovey a visit and deliver their gifts. Knowing Duncan was on his way back home from Boston, she didn't want to linger. She used the excuse she was tired and jetlagged (although this was adamantly true) and she had work to do in the morning preparing for the annual arrival of the autumn tourists. It was now after nine o'clock and her house was quiet, which was something that she used to relish. Tatiana was used to a life alone, but after spending time with Hamish, and especially the utterly adorable Lachlan, she astonishingly found herself lonely. Lonely for Hamish's embrace, for their afternoon ritual of tea and scones, for their long walks in the Highlands, and for chasing after a very active toddler.

Being part of the Falconer everyday life had made her feel like she had lived there forever. The sight of Hamish's house near St. Andrew's Links, the home of many British Opens, captivated her instantly. While Hamish wished to take her on a "proper" sight-seeing tour, she found joy in staying at his home, wandering the glens, and exploring the village shops and pubs nearby. This hadn't been a touristy type of visit for Tatiana by any means; it was a visit to spend time and to reconnect with the man she had fallen in love with so many years ago. Hamish was the only man Tatiana had ever loved—he was her one and only true love. And reconnect they did, catching up on the decades over endless cups of chai tea and cinnamon scones. She got to know Colin, the spitting image of Hamish in his youth, and his darling wife Haleigh, the quin-tessential Scottish lass with hair the color of autumn chestnuts and eyes as green as the sea. Haleigh's devotion to her family was evident to Tatiana with her wonderful home-cooked Irish stews and congenial hospitality. Lachlan was the perfect combination of his parents—hair as dark as Colin's, and eyes as green as fresh kiwis like Haleigh's. Hamish made the little family complete and Tatiana never felt unwelcome. The Falconer family lovingly embraced her, making her feel like an honorary member.

And now, here she was alone in Maine. She tried to cheer herself up by making tea, but the instant it hit her tongue, it tasted bitter. When she and Hamish discussed how they would continue their long-distance relationship, a seasonal back-and-forth flight schedule seemed the perfect solution. It sounded like a good plan in Scotland, but now that she was home and back to the reality of her life, the only thing she could think of was Hamish.

"You wanted this, silly," she said as she dumped her tea into the sink. She threw the blue tartan wrap around her shoulders. It was a gift from Hamish, and Tatiana swore she could smell the cold clean air of the Highlands within its cashmere. She pulled it tighter under her chin and imagined that the shawl that now embraced her was the loving arms of Hamish. She padded downstairs from her apartment to the gallery. She turned on the switch, and the little gallery was aglow in soft yellow light. It brought a smile to Tatiana's face, as she genuinely missed The Blue Hydrangea. Her eyes landed upon the beautiful painting of Annabelle. Like Lachlan, Annabelle was the perfect blend of Tatiana and Hamish, with Hamish's dark blueberry-colored eyes, and Tatiana's hair as yellow as daffodils. Annabelle. The enchanting little girl she and Hamish created after one serendipitous night together. Tatiana no longer cried when she looked at the ethereal portrait Hamish commissioned for her, especially now that she and Hamish had become reacquainted. Albeit short, Annabelle's life was a life full of love— love that was showered upon her by her father and adoptive mother. Even though Tatiana did not raise the child she gave birth to, she always felt there was an unbreakable connection between a mother and her child, and she knew Hamish would take the utmost care of her. He and Hannah most certainly did.

"Sweet child," Tatiana whispered. She put a kiss to her fingers and gently let the kiss touch the child's chubby pink cheek in the painting. Tatiana never thought that at her age she would find herself at a crossroads. Did she truly love Lobster Claw enough to stay? She couldn't even believe such a thought crossed her mind, but it did—and not just now. It had also crossed her mind in Scotland, while with Hamish and his family. She never brought up to Hamish the possibility of her selling The Blue Hydrangea, giving up everything and moving to Scotland to be with him, which she had considered.

"Would that even be plausible? Could I truly do something like that?" she asked, still gazing at Annabelle. She had lost so much—Hamish, Annabelle. Now, after some miracle had returned Hamish to her, she did not want to lose him again. No, Hamish was more important than a gallery, and perhaps even more important than her life in her beloved Lobster Claw.

Tatiana's body grew heavy, her eyelids drooping as weariness washed over her. The weight of her thoughts consumed her mind and body, and she needed sleep. After enduring such a long journey, so many impossible-to-answer questions swirled in her mind like a fierce storm, tangling her weary mind, and her body begged for rest.

"Not tonight," she said, turning off the light in the gallery, ascending the stairs back to her apartment. She had been so happy, but returning home, she now felt torn. What to do? Here or there? Both? "Tatiana, stop it," she scolded. "It's too late, and you are beyond exhausted. Get yourself to bed. There's plenty of time to think about this tomorrow." She lugged her fatigued body up the stairs to her bedroom and collapsed on her bed. She just wanted to sleep, to sleep away any decision about what she would do in this next chapter of her life—to stay or to leave her cherished Lobster Claw, Maine, for love.

CHAPTER 8

WITH TREMBLING HANDS

Charlotte wrapped her new tartan shawl about her shoulders and stepped out in the chilly October morning to let Lovey out in the yard. It was a little too cool for a walk on the beach with Lovey, so the yard would have to do. Later, when the sun warmed the day, she would grab Tatiana, and the three would have their beach walk.

"You behave, sweetie," Charlotte said to her dog as she hurried back inside. Lovey didn't seem to mind the cold at all and loved her little backyard. She would stalk field mice and chipmunks that were just as fast as the whitecaps Lovey also loved to chase, but of course, never caught. Even though the small patch of yard had a secure fence, Charlotte always watched Lovey through the kitchen window to ensure her safety, just as she was doing now—running back into the kitchen and peeking out the window. Lovey was lying on the brown grass, with a reddish-brown leaf tucked between her paws.

"She can make a toy of anything," Charlotte said with a laugh, her mind now getting back to the task at hand—coffee and more online catalogues. Her eye then suddenly caught the chocolate box on her coffee table. She had restrained herself and indulged in just one chocolate last night, though she wanted to devour at least half the box. Besides, there was too much to catch up with Duncan. It wasn't until close to two o'clock in the morning that Charlotte shooed him into his truck and back to his home.

The weekend was almost there, and they'd be busy with the leaf peepers arriving, clamoring for the quaint charm of autumn that only a coastal town can bring. The waves at the beach were huge, and surfers came to Lobster Claw every fall, making Harry's Surf and Turf even busier and more profitable, which thrilled Harry.

Charlotte looked out her window toward Sand Dollar Drive. She relished her and Lovey's daily walks, marveling at the sight of the majestic oaks, their leaves that transformed into breathtaking works of art, with vibrant, blazing colors that only Mother Nature could create. The smell of the crisp scent of autumn filled the air, and the leaves would gently rustle under her feet. Charlotte was in awe of the sheer beauty that surrounded her, and Lobster Claw gave her a perpetual sense of tranquility. She was no stranger to stunning New England autumns from her time at Castle Loch, but the colors of a Maine fall were dazzling, with reds that were as bright as rubies, and gold as shiny as Rapunzel's hair. Geese in perfect V formations took flight into the azure blue sky, and ducks waddled into small ponds searching for their next meal. Charlotte felt the enchanting Lobster Claw trails could lead to a real Narnia, a fairyland just beyond the trees. However, much to Charlotte's relief and delight, they always found themselves on the wooded path leading to the back of Elsie's Everything, where she and Lovey would stop in for coffee and a dog biscuit.

But today was not a day for a walk through the mystical woods of Lobster Claw, Maine. Today was a day for work—getting ready for Thanksgiving and the Christmas season, as Snow Cap Mountain was close by and, according to Elsie, "always has snow for the holidays!" The exit to Snow Cap was next to Sand Dollar Drive, so naturally, skiers, snowboarders, and ice skaters who headed for the resort always veered into Lobster Claw. Take the Cake had special holiday treats ready, and at The Blue Hydrangea, beautiful winterscapes of Northern Maine flew off the walls.

Charlotte ordered some gloves that had tiny lobsters on the forefinger and thumb that were tacky for texting ability. As she snuggled into her Scottish shawl, she thought about ordering some shawls to see how they would sell. With her retail management sixth sense, Charlotte had the distinct feeling the shawls would do very well, and she made a mental note to text Hamish later about ordering some. She also acquired unique blends of coffee to accommodate the changing seasons—an autumn blend from a coffee roaster in Camden, as well as other blends with notes of cinnamon, cocoa, and rustic spices. The festive coffee was perfect for the Christmas season, and she would also order hot chocolate from a local chocolatier.

Charlotte's excitement for the holidays grew with each idea, but the familiar sound of a black pickup truck rolling into the driveway, along with Lovey's excited barks, interrupted her merchandising thoughts. Charlotte pulled the shawl tighter over her shoulders and let Lovey inside, and the two of them went through the front door to greet Duncan.

"My two favorite girls," he said, a smile beaming on his days-old bearded face, which Charlotte found quite attractive. Charlotte saw his hand slip into the pocket of his leather bomber jacket. "Who's my good girl?" he said, laughing as Lovey obediently sat in front of him. He gently gave her a bone-shaped dog cookie. Lovey gingerly took it from his hand and then dropped it on the ground. She quickly kissed Duncan's hand, picked up the treat, and charged into the house and onto her bed where she could enjoy it.

"I know, I know," he said, his arms outstretched toward Charlotte. She felt those strong arms ensconce her in a hug. "Too many treats," he whispered, and Charlotte felt his kiss on her waiting lips.

Her heart raced, and her hands trembled as if it was their first kiss. She prayed she would always feel this way, that all their kisses would feel like their first. Charlotte would never grow tired of feeling his lips upon hers. She snuggled into him as her shawl dropped from her shoulders. Duncan retrieved it and wrapped it around her.

"Thank you," she said, feeling his arms tighten around the shawl.

"So, ready to tackle our new venture?" he asked. His protective arm was around her as they headed into the bungalow. Back in the warmth of the cottage, she carefully folded the shawl and placed it on the back of the couch.

"You know I am, and there's plenty of coffee, too," she said, walking into the kitchen and grabbing mugs from the cabinet. She poured each of them a cup of the aromatic coffee and brought them to the coffee table, along with some croissants she picked up from Take the Cake.

"Amazing." He made himself comfortable on the old couch and took a sip of the coffee. "Oh, I left something in the truck," he said, putting his mug down and jumping up from the couch. "Alfred and William had a huge envelope for me. I think it has something to do with the Newport project. Let me run and get it. Be right back."

A cold breeze blew in the bungalow from the opened door. "Brrr," she whispered.

Sometimes, the happiness in her life scared her, considering it was once taken away from her painfully. However, the shawl and the person who gifted it to her, served as a reminder to Charlotte of the security she now had in amazing friends and a supportive community in Lobster Claw, along with her love for Duncan.

"Wow, it's cold out there," he said, jogging through the still-open door with the envelope under his arm. He closed the door, returned to the couch and sipped his coffee. He then carefully tore the top of the envelope.

"Alfred and William are so excited about this Newport

project," he began. He pulled out a crisp sheet of paper from the envelope and he read as he spoke. "Hey, what do you think about heading down there for a long weekend? I haven't been in years . . ." Duncan suddenly stopped speaking.

Charlotte sat next to him and watched his face contort in consternation as he read the contents of a letter. She saw his healthy, ruddy face whiten as he solely focused on the letter in his hand.

"What is it, Duncan?" Charlotte asked, sipping her coffee. "Are those two up to their old tricks trying to get you to do more than you bargained for?" She feigned a smile as a slight twist in her gut told her the letter had nothing to do with William and Alfred.

"No," Duncan said.

Charlotte saw the letter shake within his trembling hands. She heard the huskiness and severity in his voice, and the small wrench in her stomach was now more like a vice, tightening with anxiety at each passing second.

"I think you need to read this as well," Duncan said.

Charlotte took the letter from his quivering hands.

CHAPTER 9

YOURS IN HEAVEN

"I don't know what to say," Charlotte said with a sigh, handing the letter back to Duncan.

"That makes two of us," Duncan replied, holding the letter in his hands and reading it again.

"You had no idea?" She put her arm around him, trying to provide comfort to Duncan, who shook from the astonishing news that was contained in the letter. "Do you mind if I read it again?" she asked softly.

"Of course not," he said, handing her the letter.

Charlotte read the letter aloud in a whispered tone.

Dear Mr. Kirk,

Allow me to introduce myself. My name is Samuel Reese, a family practice attorney based in Newport, Rhode Island.

My client, Isobel Frost, retained my services when she discovered she had an inoperable brain tumor. Ms. Frost is the mother of an eight-year-old daughter, Edwina (Wini) Frost. When Ms. Frost realized she would not survive her illness, she requested my help in ensuring all legal procedures were followed for her young daughter. Ms. Frost has made her aunt, Crystal Frost, the legal guardian of

*Wini. However, Ms. Frost wanted it made known, legally, the iden-
tity of Wini's biological father, and she has named you.*

*Enclosed with this letter, you will find all the documentation
pertaining to Ms. Frost's claims, and procedures on how you would
dispute this, if that is what you seek.*

*I will note that Ms. Frost is NOT making any demands, finan-
cial or personal, on you—she simply wanted you to know that you
have a daughter.*

*Besides legal documentation, there is a letter from Ms. Frost
which she wanted to make sure you received.*

*Please contact me and I am more than happy to video conference
with you, or if you prefer, I am also available for an in-house
appointment as well.*

Sincerely,
Samuel Reese, Esq.
Samuel Reese Family Law
Newport, Rhode Island

Charlotte then noticed a blue envelope peeking out from the rest
of the documentation. She pulled it out and saw that the envelope
simply had "Duncan" written on it.

"This must be that letter," Charlotte said.

She handed Duncan the envelope and watched him slowly
open it and pull out a white sheet of paper. He then read aloud:

Dear Duncan,

*If you are reading this letter, it means that I am no longer of this
world, and am hopefully with the angels. I have no doubt the
contents of this package shocked you, but it is absolutely true—you
have a daughter. And a beautiful one at that.*

I knew when I first met you that you were not "the one," and I know you felt that about me, too. But who could resist those dancing hazel eyes and the thousand-watt smile that just lit up the room? You were handsome, exciting, and a wonderful diversion for me at a time in my life when I most needed it. When I discovered I was pregnant, I returned to Rhode Island. I was ready for this baby, but I knew you were not. I had the financial means to take care of a baby, and I wanted no strings attached. I felt there was no reason to pressure you with a child; so, I didn't. But over the years, as Wini grew, I knew I was wrong. When I discovered I had an inoperable brain tumor that would eventually claim me, that is when I decided to put things to right, hence the documentation from Mr. Reese, my attorney.

Wini is in the legal custody of my aunt Crystal, who loves her deeply and who has been like a second mother herself. But Wini has a father.

I am sorry you are discovering this momentous news in such a fashion, but I also never imagined I would face a death sentence before I was forty-five.

I will leave it absolutely up to you if you want to proceed and meet Wini, and if you do not, I would totally understand. I can rest in peace now with a clear conscience.

Yours in heaven,
Isobel Frost

Charlotte noticed the silhouette of a small square tucked within the envelope. She pulled out a photograph—the type that schools take every year, with the same blue background that Charlotte had when she was a child. She looked at the photograph and sighed. "Oh, Duncan," she murmured, handing him the photograph. His hand shook as he took the photo.

"Charlotte," he barely whispered.

"I know," she said, enveloping him in a comforting embrace.

The photo staring back at them was the female replica of

Duncan. Wini had the same dancing hazel eyes and a deep dimple in her squared-off chin. They had the same straight nose and prominent forehead. The only difference was that Wini had long, straight, strawberry blonde hair, and although her eyebrows were similar in shape to Duncan's, they matched the color of her hair.

"She looks just like my mother," Duncan whispered, his eyes never leaving the picture of the girl.

"She looks just like you." Charlotte tightened her grip around him. His body was tense and rigid. Charlotte kissed his hot cheek. "Are you okay?" she asked gently. "I know it's a stupid question, but . . ."

"I just don't know what to say. I just did not know." He put his head into his hands and Charlotte felt his body shake with sobs.

"Duncan," Charlotte said softly, pulling him closer to her, gently kissing his stubbled cheek. She felt his hand strongly grip onto hers, tightening, as if she were a life preserver, and he was clinging on for dear life.

"I had no idea. No idea at all," he said.

As Duncan's sobs subsided, Charlotte felt him relax against the worn couch cushions. She gently brushed away the tears that streamed onto his cheeks from his red and sorrowful eyes.

"If I had known, I would have helped. I would have taken care of her. Of them."

"Of course you would have," Charlotte said. "But you didn't know. Her mother didn't want you to know. That was her decision. But she also knew that decision was not the right one. Do you remember Isobel?"

He blew a loud sigh of resignation. "I do remember her. It was a couple of years before I met Melinda. We met at some kind of work function. She was a wedding event planner, doing very well for herself, as I recall. I remembered seeing this stunning woman with long and wavy red hair. We were in one of those rooftop restaurants. It was spring and there was an enclosed balcony. She was by herself, nursing a drink. Anyway, I couldn't understand how someone that attractive was alone, so I walked my cocky self right up to her, introduced myself, and asked her to be my date for the evening. She had this dazzling smile and green twinkling eyes to match." He paused. "I'm sorry, I don't mean to sound—"

"You don't sound like anything," Charlotte said. Talking about Isobel seemed to relax him a bit, as she saw his shoulders slacken. "We're both in our fifties now, and we both have pasts. Yours might be a little more checkered than mine," she said with a laugh, watching a smile form on his face. "You had a life before me, and I had one before you. But," she said, wrapping her arms around him, "we're together now, and you can tell me anything. But that's sweet of you to consider my feelings."

As his body leaned into hers, she could see the tenderness in his eyes. At the touch of his lips upon hers, Charlotte's eyes closed, and a quiver pulsated through her body. She felt the depth of his love through his kiss.

"I don't know what I'd do without you," Duncan said. "Especially now."

Charlotte shook her head. "You're never going to find out. We'll figure this out. Together." She softly kissed his cheek. "Now, tell me about her. She sounds stunningly beautiful."

Duncan laughed, and his eyes crinkled with his smile. "She was. She was up for any kind of adventure, too. We actually flew to Paris just for a weekend once. She wrote it off as a business expense. I liked her a lot. She was fun, spontaneous, adventurous. But I also knew, like she said, that she wasn't 'the one.' I knew she didn't feel that way about me, either. It was a summer fling, and then one day, she said she wanted to move her business to Newport. She was going after a different sort of clientele, and being from there, she knew the area, the people, the venues. At first I thought she was crazy for leaving Boston, but I got it—Newport is uber wealthy, and she wanted to break into the market. It was actually a smart move on her part. We texted a couple of times. You know, she saying she'd come up here for a weekend, and vice versa, but it never happened. I figured she moved on with her life. Boy, she certainly did. She never let on that she was pregnant, but I guess she didn't want me—just the baby."

"Do you think that's all she wanted from you?" Charlotte felt bad, as if someone had taken advantage of Duncan for all the wrong reasons.

"No, no, I don't. She never mentioned children, marriage, you know, like most women her age did. I don't want to sound pretentious, but it's especially true when they start dating a successful, somewhat older man. I was about ten years older than her, so she would have been around thirty-five—that age when some women who haven't been married or had children desperately want it. But she wasn't like that. From what I could see, she completely focused on her career, and I respected that."

"I think I know how she felt," Charlotte said. "I said nothing to Landon, but I always secretly hoped I would get pregnant. I knew I was getting older, and the window was closing, but if it happened, I know it would have made me the happiest woman on Earth—to have a baby with him." She choked back her own tears. "I never told anyone that, not even Landon. I was afraid if I did . . ."

"That might scare him?" Duncan asked softly. Charlotte nestled into his chest.

"I'm not sure it would have scared him, but I was always afraid if I mentioned children, things between us could change. It's hard to articulate, actually. He felt his life was perfect the way it was, and he was so happy with Peppercorn." Charlotte pulled away, shrugged and shook her head. "I think I understand Isobel. Maybe she knew her window was closing too, and she just got lucky enough. She knew you didn't truly love her, or her you, so she made it easier for everyone. Like she said in her letter, she never thought in a million years she'd leave her daughter motherless. I'll bet it was absolutely devastating for her."

"I'm sure you're right. When are you not?" He smelled the clean scent of her shampoo as he leaned in and gently kissed the top of her head. "The question now is, what do I do?"

"I think you already know," Charlotte said, looking at Wini's photo.

CHAPTER 10

GREAT COMFORT

Crystal Frost sat at her kitchen table drinking a cup of decaffeinated green tea. She would have preferred strong black coffee, but at three o'clock in the afternoon, she knew the powerful punch of caffeine would keep her up at night. And nighttime was when all of Crystal's doubts and fears materialized before her eyes and inside of her brain—doubts and fears about raising an eight-year-old child at age sixty-five. Truth be told, Crystal didn't feel any differently than she did at forty-five—she suffered from no aches and pains like most of her contemporaries were complaining of at this stage of life. She had no diabetes, no thyroid issues, and was on no medications, which always surprised the ever-revolving round of medical assistants who took her history and blood pressure prior to her annual physical.

While all that was true, the fact was that she was on her way to seventy. She'd watched her niece, Isobel, grow from babyhood to adulthood, and she knew how fast the years breezed by.

"Too fast," she said, getting up to look out of the window to see if the school bus had arrived.

No matter what time of the year, Newport, Rhode Island, was always beautiful. In the rear of her house were spectacular views of the ocean, and in the front, the leaves of gargantuan maples that lined her cul-de-sac were now the perennial colors of a New England autumn: ruby red, golden yellow, and russet brown. Pumpkins, haystacks, and scarecrows adorned the homes that dotted the cul-de-sac. Halloween was next week, and it would mark the five-month anniversary of Isobel's death. Crystal was always thankful that when Isobel discovered she was pregnant, she returned to Newport and lived with her in the family home, making Wini the fourth generation to live in it. Isobel's parents had passed, so the house solely belonged to Crystal.

Crystal remained unmarried, and the three Frost girls lived happily together until Isobel received a diagnosis of glioblastoma. She passed away within three months of receiving her diagnosis. Although she had prepared Wini well, and was open and honest, Isobel and Crystal maintained to keep Wini's routine as ordinary as possible. But now and then, when Crystal gave into those three o'clock coffee urges, and she was up late, she could hear Wini crying.

Crystal would comfort her grandniece as much as she could, but she knew Wini missed her mother terribly, despite the brave face the young girl always put on. But because of the type of mother Isobel was, Crystal knew Wini adjusted to her mother's death more easily than others. Isobel always told her that anytime a feather would land near her, or if Wini heard a cardinal sing, or if she saw a shooting star, that would mean Isobel was near. Fortunately, the flora and fauna of their backyard attracted many cardinals, and the occasional feather would fall, seemingly out of nowhere, landing near Wini. A look of joy would spread across her face as she took comfort in knowing her mother was near.

Crystal returned to the table and pulled the letter from Samuel Reese, Esq. from its envelope. The letter arrived this morning and stated that Isobel proclaimed Duncan Kirk as Wini's biological father, and the lawyer had sent all the documentation to him. Isobel wanted this man to know that he had a daughter, which

Crystal well understood. But Wini had so much upheaval in the past few months, Crystal worried about Duncan suddenly appearing and disrupting Wini's life.

Isobel had told Crystal about her pregnancy when she returned to Newport, and who the father was, as well as her decision to have the baby on her own. Unbeknownst to Isobel, Crystal followed Duncan through these last eight years via social media and knew more about Duncan's professional life than probably his own mother did. It brought her pride to see Isobel choose to keep the baby and not go after Duncan. Isobel believed in true love, and her true love was not that man. Isobel's true love was her very own daughter.

Crystal knew her niece explained to Wini that she had a father, and that an angel told Isobel that Wini would meet her father one day, but not right now. Satisfied with this, Wini never gave her father a second thought, and the three of them lived happily for eight blissful years.

But now the harsh reality of death settled over the Frost household. There was the looming fact that Duncan Kirk might appear and want to meet his daughter, and if he did, it would give Crystal the answer to the question she had been asking herself—is he good enough a person to be in Wini's life? Just because Duncan was professionally successful didn't mean that he was a good man personally. But Crystal would know. If he contacted her about possibly meeting Wini, Crystal's incredible intuition would signal if he was up to the task. But that day might never come. Or it could come all too soon.

"The heck with it," Crystal said, getting up from the table. "I need that coffee desperately." She was just about to pour the dark coffee grounds into the coffeemaker when the loud screech of the school bus brakes interrupted her. She put down the canister, and happy as a schoolchild herself, Crystal ran out the front door to greet her grandniece.

CHAPTER 11

TWO GOOD MEN

"That's incredible," Tatiana said as she helped Charlotte store the autumnal merchandise in the basement.

All too suddenly, the calendar had turned from October to November, and it was time to decorate for Christmas. It was a chilly day with no sun to speak of, but Tatiana's bright smile lit up the darkened Shop at Beach Rose Path. Charlotte desperately needed some sunshine in her life, and Tatiana could always provide that.

"Isn't it?" Charlotte said, packing up the last of the Rubbermaid containers full of leaf garlands, pumpkins, skeletons, and ghouls.

"What's Duncan thinking?" Tatiana asked as she sat down on the shop's couch. "Let's take a little break and chat." She patted the empty cushion next to her, motioning Charlotte to sit as Lovey napped on her bed near the door.

"He's planning on meeting her. And he wants me to go with him." Charlotte sipped dark, rich coffee and immediately felt the kick she needed.

"How do you feel about that?" Tatiana gently asked.

"You know I would do anything for Duncan, but I told him I

thought it was better that he meet her by himself. But he said we're a team, and that he wanted me to be there, as this will affect my life as well." Charlotte put the cup on the table and looked at Tatiana.

"It will," Tatiana said. "It's quite monumental. I know." Decades ago, Tatiana had kept a similar secret from Hamish.

Charlotte smiled at her friend. "Yes, you do know. But it was different for you. When you were expecting, you told Hamish. But this Isobel dropped quite the bomb on Duncan, informing him he had a daughter. She's eight and now motherless. I feel like a character in a soap opera," Charlotte said with a laugh to keep the tears from falling, although she did not find the situation funny at all. If truth be told, she was heartsick. The anxiety she thought was dead and buried from when she'd lost Landon and Peppercorn was resurfacing. Her deep-seated fear that she could lose Duncan was causing her sleepless nights.

Charlotte felt Tatiana's soft and comforting hands gently clasp about hers.

"Charlotte, life can be a soap opera, believe you me. And I think Duncan is right—that you should be there when he meets her. He's going to need you, and I think if this little girl also sees a female presence, it might make it easier for her. You are so good with children. And dogs. It might even be a good idea for Lovey to go along. Animals are the best icebreakers."

"I thought of that," Charlotte said, casting a glance at her own sleeping bundle of joy. "Duncan did too. We're set to drive down on Saturday."

"You seem a little unsure," Tatiana said, stroking Charlotte's arm, reminding her of her own mother's comforting touch.

"I am. I think I'm more nervous about Duncan. I guess I don't really know what to think. One thing I do know, I am glad that he wants to meet her. It makes him even more special to me. We'll figure all this out together."

"You absolutely will," Tatiana said, pulling Charlotte close.

"Duncan is a good man. He's not hesitating. He's grabbing this bull by the horns and doing what a man needs to do."

"Like Hamish did áll those years ago," Charlotte said softly, knowing that was what her friend was thinking.

"Exactly," Tatiana murmured. A wave of emotion suddenly washed over her, and she felt tears sting her eyes.

"We are so lucky to have these two good men in our lives, Charlotte."

"No tears," Charlotte commanded, rising from the couch.

Lovey awoke with a stretch and wandered toward the door, a signal she was ready to take a stroll by the beach.

"Come on," Charlotte said, "time for Lovey's walk. We can talk some more while she splashes in the surf."

"The cold air will do us both some good," Tatiana agreed as they grabbed their jackets and the three headed out for a much needed beach walk.

CHAPTER 12

NICELY DONE

"I don't even know what to say." Ivy was sitting behind her desk at her veterinary practice.

Duncan sat on the other side of his sister's desk, shrugging his shoulders. "I'm still in shock myself. Charlotte and I are driving down on Saturday to meet Wini and her grandaunt, Crystal."

"Already? That's moving pretty fast. Don't you want to think this over a little? I mean—"

"I have thought it over, Iv," Duncan said as he stood and walked over to one of the crates in Ivy's office where a small kitten was peacefully sleeping. "If I think about it any longer, well, then I might change my mind. I mean, look at her."

Ivy picked up the photo that Duncan had brought. "I know. She looks just like Mom except for the red hair." She sighed, shaking her head, still looking at the photograph. "I hate to ask, but I will. You do plan to have a DNA test done, right? Just to be certain?" Even from Wini's photo, Ivy knew there was no mistake in that she was Duncan's daughter, but Ivy played things safer than Duncan did.

He sighed heavily and shook his head. "I thought about that, but c'mon, Ivy, the resemblance is indisputable. You even said so yourself."

"Well," Ivy said, standing from her chair, and gaining her balance with her hands on her belly, then walking over to her big brother, "you just never know what life is going to throw at us Kirks." She wrapped one arm about Duncan's shoulders as the other still laid protectively across her baby. "I wanted a baby so much and I didn't think it would ever happen. And now look at me. And you. Two surprises." Ivy smiled, hugging her brother tighter.

"Oh, speaking of surprises," Duncan said, slowly pulling away from her embrace. "I have something else to tell you."

"Please, you're about to put me into early labor. Let me sit again down and brace myself," she said with a laugh, sitting on a stool near the stack of pet crates.

Duncan pulled the small black velvet box from the inside pocket of his bomber jacket and handed it to her.

"Oh, you shouldn't have." She laughed, slowly opening the box. "Oh, Duncan, it's beautiful. Is this what I think it is?" she asked, handing the box back to Duncan.

"What do you think it is?" he asked his sister mischievously.

"C'mon, big brother," Ivy laughed, reaching up and punching him in his arm. "That's an engagement ring if I ever saw one. It's stunning, Duncan. Who knew you had such elegant taste?"

"I had a little help," he said, taking it from her and putting it back into his pocket.

"Well, nicely done. So, when are you going to pop the proverbial question? I promise I won't tell a soul. Well, maybe Andy, but you know how close mouthed he is."

Keeping secrets was Ivy's specialty, and she'd proved herself to be a valuable ally when they were younger by helping Duncan sneak out of the house undetected by their parents.

He shook his head. "I don't know. Not yet, but soon. I think I'll know when the time comes."

Ivy smiled lovingly at him.

"Our little Kirk family is getting bigger by the minute," she said, laughing.

Duncan squeezed his sister's shoulder. "You're about to be a mother, and me a father. And a husband . . ."

"And an uncle," Ivy added. "Mom and Dad would be thrilled."

"Well, maybe not so much with me. I didn't even know this little girl existed until now." Duncan's voice dipped in shame. "I feel like I let down Mom and Dad, only thinking about myself and my own good times, and that I was arrogant enough to think this would never happen."

"Mom and Dad would have accepted and loved her. You know about her now, and that's what matters." Ivy comfortingly patted his arm. "Charlotte will be with you," Ivy began softly. "It's just like me and Andy—you can do anything together. She'll help you, Duncan."

"She will. Do you think she'll like the ring?" Duncan asked.

"She won't like it—she will love it." Ivy's excitement was evident from the joy in her voice and the smile on her face. "And that is one thing I know for sure." Ivy quickly stood up and grimaced.

"Are you okay?" Duncan asked, concerned at the sudden change in Ivy's expression.

"Oh, Duncan," she whispered, grabbing his hand and lightly placing it on her belly.

"Ivy! The baby!" Duncan shouted, feeling a tiny movement underneath his hand.

"That's your niece or nephew," Ivy murmured, as tears formed in her eyes. She put her hand on the other side.

"I've never felt anything like that before in my life, Ivy," Duncan said softly.

"Kind of puts things into perspective, doesn't it?" she said quietly.

"It does. Even though Wini is eight, she was once kicking

inside of Isobel. I wasn't there then, but I am now, and I'm not going to screw this up. I'm determined to be there for her. And for this little one, too."

"I know you will be. I couldn't ask for a better brother, and this baby is nothing but blessed having you as an uncle. And I know one day Wini will be saying the same thing about you—what a wonderful father you are."

"I hope you're right," Duncan said.

"She will."

Duncan kissed his sister on her forehead. He had felt nothing like this in his life, and that one fetal kick put his own life into perspective. He had a child, too. Albeit, she was now eight years old and far from an infant, but feeling his sister's baby move in her belly brought it all home to Duncan. Biologically, he was a father, but more importantly, he wanted to be a physical father as well to the daughter he just discovered. After spending time with his sister and her unborn baby, he was determined now, more than ever, to be just that.

CHAPTER 13

ROAD TRIP

"Okay, Lovey, that's the last of it." Charlotte finished packing her bag for the trip to Newport. She had a separate one for Lovey as well, containing her food, water bowl, and dog bed. Duncan's truck was big enough to fit everything, and they were ready for their road trip.

"Oh, gosh, one more thing," she said, as she ran upstairs to her bedroom loft. Charlotte did not want to meet Wini and her grandaunt empty-handed, so she had gotten them each a gift. She chose a painting from The Blue Hydrangea of Sea Star Lighthouse for Crystal. Not exactly sure what to buy for an eight-year-old girl, Charlotte had asked the opinion of Take the Cake's Betsy's ten-year-old granddaughter, who thought the young girl would love a pink hooded sweatshirt with Lobster Claw, Maine emblazoned on the front.

Giving the place one last glance, she felt satisfied that she had everything and waited for Duncan to arrive. At the familiar roar of his car, Lovey started jumping wildly, knowing that Duncan had arrived.

"Okay, okay, sweetie," Charlotte said. Her head pounded with anxiety and a nervous tension gripped her stomach. She inhaled deeply, remembering the breathing exercises she used when pangs of panic descended upon her. After a couple of moments of deep breathing, she started to feel relief, and the anxiety subsided. She watched Duncan get out of his truck, and the confident air in his stride relaxed her even more. *You are going because the man you love needs you,* Charlotte thought. *Yes, it's all very unorthodox, but here you are.*

Charlotte opened the door and Lovey wildly escaped, jumping on Duncan and greeting him in the only way she could. The cold, clean air filled Charlotte's lungs, her head cleared, and she felt at peace. At least for now.

Duncan opened the passenger door of his truck, and Lovey hopped right in. He shut the door and headed right toward Charlotte. "Ready?" he asked, greeting her with a loving kiss.

"I am," she whispered, feeling more confident in herself now that Duncan was by her side.

"This it?" he asked, nodding at her weekend bag and two totes —one that contained Lovey's things and one that contained the gifts.

"I travel light," she said with a smile, watching Duncan pick up the bags and head to the truck.

An odd sense of melancholy nabbed Charlotte as she was about to lock the bungalow door. She realized that since May, she'd been nowhere else. There was no place she'd rather be. Her home in Lobster Claw was perfect, and why would she want to leave paradise? "We'll see you tomorrow," she said softly to the bungalow, an assurance to herself as well that this brief trip was just temporary, and before she knew it, she and Lovey would be back home. Charlotte locked up, joined Duncan in the truck, and they were on their way down Sand Dollar Drive and to a little girl who, Charlotte hoped, needed her father.

CHAPTER 14

A BABY

"This person is really my dad, Aunt Crys?" Edwina Frost sat at the kitchen table finishing up a bowl of apple-cinnamon Cheerios. Small seed pearls were sewn into the collar and cuffs of the mint-colored sweater she was wearing. She wore a denim skirt with navy blue tights and a pair of blue booties. A ribbon, matching her sweater, tied her golden red hair in a long, silky ponytail. Tiny emerald studs shimmered on her earlobes, a gift from her mother on Wini's last birthday that glimmered in the early afternoon sunshine.

Crystal was beyond surprised that she heard from Duncan so quickly, and when he said he wanted to visit with his significant other, as he put it, she was at a loss. Although Crystal knew all about his professional life, she had to admit that when she spoke to him on the phone, he seemed genuine with his intentions about Wini. Genuine or not, this would not be easy, and Crystal didn't know who it might be harder on—her or Wini.

Isobel had always been an open book, and she was straightforward with Wini about her father. She'd loved to weave magical stories for her daughter, and Crystal recalled the story she told Wini.

Crystal turned and looked at the fire burning brightly in the fireplace, taking her back to one winter evening, when Wini was six. The snow had been falling lightly that January night, and inside the living room, a fire was blazing in the fireplace. They sat together, sipping hot chocolate and watching the snow fall. And that's when Isobel spun Wini the most spellbinding fairy tale about her father.

"One day," Isobel began, "Mommy met a very special man. We liked each other very much. It was at a time, sweetie, when Mommy wanted only one thing. And that was a baby."

"Me!" Wini proudly sung upon hearing what Isobel wanted.

"That's right," Isobel continued. "Now, like I said, this man was very special. And he was a very busy man, too. We were walking in the countryside and talking, and he asked me what would be the one thing that would make me happy. And my answer was a baby. He laughed and told me he didn't think he could help me with that wish, but I didn't care that he thought it was funny. That was my wish. One day, this man—"

"What was his name, Mommy?" Wini asked, her eyes full of wonderment at the story her mother was spinning, sipping her hot chocolate.

"His name was Duncan."

"Like Duncan Donuts," Wini said, laughing.

"Yes. Like Duncan Donuts. Well, one day, Duncan told me he had to go on a very long trip and that he did not know when he would return. I was very sad that he was leaving, but he said he needed to go for his job. I understood his situation, and I told him I was so happy that I got to meet him and to get to know him. He told me he was happy to know me too, and that he had hoped that someday my wish would come true. Well, not too long after that, my wish did come true. And here you are."

"So Duncan helped make your wish come true," Wini said matter-of-factly. "And because he did that, that makes him my father?"

"Yes, Wini. Because he helped me with my wish that makes him your father," Isobel replied, stroking her daughter's silken strawberry-blonde hair.

"Does he know about me?" Wini had asked.

"One day, he will know all about you, and I am sure that will make him very happy. You will be a very delightful surprise for him someday." Isobel pulled Wini into her lap, giving her a loving, motherly embrace.

Wini leaned in close to her mother. "I'm glad I was your wish and not anyone else's. You are the best mommy, and Auntie Crys is the best auntie."

Obviously satisfied with the answer, Wini didn't question it again, and life had gone on until Isobel's passing.

The tinkling sound of a spoon on a bowl brought Crystal back to the present. She smiled at her grandniece as she got up and wrapped her arms reassuringly around Wini's shoulders, sweetly kissing her on top of her red hair. She then took the empty bowl and put it into the dishwasher. "He is your dad, sweetie, and he wants to meet you very much."

"I remember Mommy saying I would be a happy surprise for him someday," Wini said, pouring herself a glass of chocolate milk.

Crystal looked fondly at the child. Wini's maturity always astonished Crystal. Isobel's strong belief in honesty greatly influenced Wini's resolve, despite her youth.

"You look lovely," Crystal said, bending down on her knee so she was eye to eye with her grandniece. Wini's beautiful hair and lithe body shape were so much like her mother's, and her face was that of her father. *A good combination*, Crystal thought, running her hand over Wini's pink cheek.

"Thanks. So do you," she said, laughing, "but you might want to leave this home." Wini reached behind Crystal's ear and pulled out a large pink roller.

The two Frost girls burst into laughter as Crystal grabbed the roller and threw it into the half bath off of the kitchen.

"You can't take me anywhere," Crystal said with a laugh, hugging Wini tightly. Whether meeting Duncan Donut only happened this once, or if a relationship was born, Crystal knew Wini would be fine. "Okay, let's get our coats, shall we?"

"Yup!" Wini smiled and got up from the table to put on her favorite navy blue peacoat with the gold buttons that was hanging on the back of her chair. "Let's go meet him!" Their wild laughter continued as they got into the car and drove off to meet Duncan Donut.

CHAPTER 15

THE SKI PATROL

"Ready?" Charlotte grasped onto Duncan's hand as he put the truck in park. They had stopped off at their B&B to freshen up after the long drive. Lovey was relaxed in the back seat, as if she knew she was going to be a part of something special.

"As I'll ever be," Duncan said, leaning over and kissing Charlotte.

"This looks like a cute place," she said.

They were in the parking lot of The Ski Patrol, which, according to Crystal, was Wini's favorite restaurant. The front of the eatery resembled a ski lodge, with a typical A-frame style building, large windows in the front, and a sloping roof. Skis and snowboards artistically adorned the outside of the entrance doors. There were three fire pits on the front lawn, all blazing, and guests with skewers in hand were making s'mores.

"Crystal said they were going to be on the back deck," Duncan said, glancing at his watch. "We still have about ten more minutes."

Charlotte smiled at Duncan's nervousness—he had checked his watch at least five times in the last five minutes. She could feel her own heart speed up with anticipation, as well. The child inside of this adorable restaurant could change the course of their lives. But whichever way these next few hours played out, Charlotte would be right by Duncan's side.

"Lovey is sound asleep," Charlotte said, peeking into the back seat. They had let her run at the B&B to relax her, which it certainly did. "We can leave her here for a bit, and then come back and get her. We'll just crack the windows. She'll be fine."

"Sounds good."

Duncan was fidgeting with his keys, and Charlotte noticed the slight tremble in his hand as he pulled them from the ignition. She took his hands into hers, pulled them to her lips, and kissed them.

"No need to worry," she whispered. "I'm with you."

Duncan leaned over and engulfed her in the familiar arms of his bomber jacket, something so comforting to her. "I don't know what I'd do without you. I truly don't."

"Same here. Now, come on. Let's go meet your little girl."

———

"I love it here," Charlotte said enthusiastically, thrilled by the homey decor of the restaurant. She made mental notes on the decorations, thinking of doing something similar to The Shop at Beach Rose Path for the ski season. She almost pulled out her phone to snap some photos, but thought better of it. Restaurant decor was not the reason she and Duncan were here. Yet still, the atmosphere relaxed her as she laced her arm through Duncan's.

"That must be it," Duncan said, pointing to the obvious—a large blue-and-white sign proclaiming the back deck entrance. Through a sliding glass door, they could see several patrons sitting at open fire pits with skewers full of marshmallows, along with packages of graham crackers and bars of chocolate.

"That looks like it might be them," Charlotte said, nodding toward an older woman and a young girl with beautiful reddish hair, sitting at one of the pits and laughing as the little girl spun skewered marshmallows over the open fire.

"Let's do this," Duncan said. Taking Charlotte's hand, they headed toward the sliding glass door.

Although it was hard to get a read on Duncan, upon seeing the little girl and the woman, a wave of excitement washed over Charlotte. The little girl appeared happy, and although Charlotte wasn't sure which way the day would go, she knew that their time in The Ski Patrol would be fun. She clutched the tote that contained the gifts, eager to meet Crystal and Wini Frost.

"Crystal?" asked Duncan as he and Charlotte approached the fire pit.

The older woman turned and looked up at Duncan. Her hair was chin length, cut into a smart bob, and was the color of freshly fallen snow. She was wearing a sapphire blue turtleneck, which not only accentuated her pretty hair, but her sparkling blue eyes as well. A warm and friendly smile gleamed across her face. Charlotte noticed there was no trace of apprehension or uneasiness in Crystal's demeanor, just openness and kindness.

"Charlotte, Duncan, so pleased to meet you," Crystal said, rising from her Adirondack chair in front of the fire pit. She extended her hand in greeting, first to Charlotte, and then to Duncan.

"Lovely to meet you, Crystal," Charlotte said, admiring the powerful grip of Crystal's handshake. Charlotte looked toward Duncan, who had said nothing, then Charlotte realized why. His eyes were squarely focused on Wini, who was sitting in a bright green Adirondack chair. Charlotte discretely nudged Duncan with her elbow, snapping him out of his trance.

"Crystal," he said, his smile beaming. Duncan's confidence had returned, and he not only shook Crystal's hand, but pulled her into an embrace, which she reciprocated.

"Come sit," she said, motioning back to the firepit. Charlotte and Duncan took their seats. The chairs were arranged in a circle around the pit, Duncan sitting opposite Charlotte with Crystal on his right and Wini on his left. The chairs featured extensions on their arms to serve as small tables for food and drinks.

"Wini," Crystal said gently, "this is Miss Charlotte Templeton."

Wini extended her small hand, first to Charlotte. "Nice to meet you, Miss Templeton," she said shyly.

Charlotte, quite impressed with her manners, shook her hand. "It's lovely to meet you, Miss Frost."

Charlotte detected a hint of a smile on Wini's serious face, and she was relieved. The ice was chipping away a bit although it was not yet completely broken. *That will take time*, Charlotte thought as the young girl pulled her hand away from Charlotte's.

"And this is Mr. Kirk," Crystal said as her grandniece extended her hand to her father.

"Nice to meet you, Mr. Kirk," Wini said, looking Duncan directly in the eye.

Oh boy. Charlotte grinned as she watched the overconfident and usually assertive Duncan Kirk turn to jelly. Flush rose high in his cheeks and he seemed somehow unsure of himself. Duncan's gregariousness had turned into quietness, seemingly within this young girl's hands.

"You can call me Duncan," he said, shaking Wini's hand.

Wini pulled her hand away from Duncan's and covered her mouth, trying very hard to stifle a laugh.

"I know what your name is," she said, laughing, holding her hand over her mouth. "At home, Aunt Crys and I call you Duncan Donut."

"Well, I love donuts," he said, picking up a skewer and stabbing a marshmallow. "But there is one thing that I love more." He held the marshmallow over the fire.

"S'mores!" sang Wini. "You love s'mores more. See, it even rhymes." She held her own marshmallow over the open flame.

Charlotte hadn't done this in years, so she paid careful attention to how Wini skewered the marshmallow and held it over the flame, turning it every few seconds until it was the perfect toasted brown. She then arranged the chocolate squares artistically on the graham crackers and slowly removed her marshmallow. Taking her thumb and forefinger, Wini slid the marshmallow onto the chocolate and gingerly placed the top graham cracker, pressing down carefully until the melted marshmallow oozed out on all sides. She handed the s'more to Charlotte, who gratefully accepted.

"Now I'll make one for Duncan Donut!" Wini made a s'more for him and one for Crystal, and they indulged in the messy but absolutely delicious snack.

"Oh my gosh, I almost forgot about Lovey!" Charlotte said, looking at Duncan, gooey chocolate running down his hands.

"Who is Lovey?" Wini asked, using wet wipes to clean her hands and face.

"Lovey is my dog. We brought her, but she was still sound asleep in the truck. I'm sure she's wide awake now and needs a little walk."

Wini's attention now turned from s'more making to the fact that Charlotte brought her dog. "Your dog? Oh, Aunt Crys, can I please see Lovey, too? I just love dogs, but . . ."

"If it's okay with Miss Templeton, you can," Crystal said.

"My truck is right there," Duncan said, pointing towards it. "I can even see Lovey sitting up now."

Wini looked toward the truck and waved furiously. "I see her, I see her! Miss Templeton, can I please come with you?"

Charlotte smiled at Wini's enthusiasm for Lovey. "Of course you can, but please call me Charlotte," she said.

"May I come with you, Charlotte? Please?" Wini asked again.

"Let's go. Lovey will be so happy to meet you." Charlotte extended her hand, which Wini readily grasped. "We're just right there," Charlotte said, assuring Crystal that they would be in full sight of the deck As she and Wini headed to the truck, Charlotte turned and gave Duncan a wink, which he returned with his confident smile, giving father and grandaunt some time alone.

CHAPTER 16

A NOTICEABLE SIGH

Duncan watched Charlotte and Wini walk to the truck and let Lovey out. He saw Charlotte grab one of Lovey's balls and they headed toward the small green outside of the restaurant where a couple other dogs were playing. Wini tossed the ball to Lovey, who quickly retrieved it and dropped it at Wini's feet. He could see her laugh at the excitement of Lovey's quick response. As promised, Wini looked toward the deck and waved enthusiastically at them.

"I guess this gives us time to chat a bit," Crystal said. Duncan's heart pounded in his chest, and he was sure Crystal could see his temples pulsate. Although he rarely got nervous, nerves were to be expected when someone just met their child they didn't know existed until a few weeks ago.

Duncan motioned for the waiter. "Another coffee, please. Crystal, would you like one?" He most definitely needed the comfort of his coffee for such a discussion, like the one that was about to happen.

"I'd love one, thank you," Crystal smiled. "Decaf, please."

The waiter refilled their cups, and the aroma immediately calmed him as he took a sip.

Duncan placed his cup back on the chair extension. "Wini seems well adjusted for a child who recently lost her mother."

Wini's positive reception had surprised him. It was bad enough losing your parents when you were an adult, but he could not even fathom what it would be like to lose them at her age. He knew he would not have been as well adjusted as she seemed to be.

"That was Isobel," Crystal began. "She always believed in being as forthcoming as possible about everything. When she knew she was dying, she and Wini talked about it every day. Of course, when Wini first found out, there was no consoling her, and we didn't know how much time we had left with Isobel. So, Isobel had what she called her 'Wini talks' every afternoon at four o'clock. Isobel would make a pot of tea and bake cookies, and she and Wini would talk about what would happen when Isobel, as she put it, 'went to live with the angels.' Sometimes I was part of the talks, just to let Wini know nothing would change—that we would continue to live on in our house and that I would be here for her." Crystal took a sip of her coffee. "And then there was you. You were another thing Isobel was honest with Wini about, telling her the story about how this extraordinary man granted her a most special wish—a wish for a baby. Wini never questioned it," Crystal continued. "I think that was because Isobel made sure Wini knew she had a father, and that someday they would meet. That's the only explanation I can give you for Wini's security in her life. She knows her mother is still with her in so many ways, like a guardian angel."

"Isobel must have been devastated when she learned she was sick," Duncan said. He remembered how fun and exciting Isobel was, always up for any kind of party or adventure, and how she talked about her future and her dreams.

"She was, but she remained strong because she needed Wini to be strong, too." Crystal looked straight into Duncan's eyes, and he felt her stare penetrate him to his very core. "I knew Isobel wanted you to know about Wini, but I wasn't so sure. It was not my decision to make, but I believe Isobel did the right thing when she had the lawyer draw up all the documentation. I'm still not sure—"

"Crystal," Duncan interrupted, reaching over and taking her hand in his. "When I opened that envelope from the lawyer, I was shocked. I wasn't sure what I wanted to do. And I know Isobel gave me a choice. But when I saw the photo of Wini, I felt as if I was looking at my mother." Duncan's head sank as memories of his cherished mother came rushing back.

"Your resemblance stunned me," she said. "I could see it in your photo online, but when you walked in here and I looked at you, I felt my heart skip a beat. The similarity is so uncanny." Duncan felt Crystal's grip tighten around his hand.

Crystal sighed and Duncan got a distinct feeling she was going to ask him about his intentions. He knew exactly what he was going to say.

"I have to ask. Do you want to be a part of Wini's life? She is incredibly important to me. She's gone through so much in a short period of time. If the answer is no, please tell me now so that it won't be too difficult for her."

Duncan's eyes locked with Crystal's. For a brief moment, he saw Isobel, whose eyes were just as bright, but there was also concern in Crystal's eyes, concern that Duncan wanted to allay. "More than anything, I want to be in Wini's life. My life has simmered down a bit, and that's another story for another time, but I think we can figure out how to make this work. If that's okay with you?"

There was a delay in Crystal's response, making Duncan nervous again. With a huge sigh, she released her hands from his, as if trying to make the right decision. "It is okay with me," she said quietly. "Well, look who's coming," she said with a smile as Charlotte and Wini bounded back to their firepit

"Wini just about wore Lovey out," Charlotte said, sliding into her chair and giving Duncan a reassuring smile. "She fell asleep again once she snuggled back into the car."

Despite her red face from the cold, Wini remained highly enthusiastic. "Aunt Crys, Lovey is so much fun! And she's so good. If I told her to sit for a treat, she sat right down and high five'd me."

"Well, you are a natural with dogs, and I could tell Lovey liked you very much," Charlotte said, smiling at her.

"I'm glad," Wini said, taking a sip of what was now a cold hot chocolate. But she didn't seem to mind, as she gulped it all down. "See, Aunt Crys, that means I'll make a good veterinarian someday. Can I get another hot chocolate, please?"

Duncan shot a look at Charlotte, and he knew from the sly smile that was spreading across her face exactly what he was thinking. *Veterinarian.*

"Is that what you'd like to do?" Duncan asked, gently leaning over toward her. *Genetics run deeper than just resemblances,* he thought, waiting for Wini's response.

"Yes. Once Aunt Crys and I found a baby raccoon. We brought it into the house and wrapped it in a blanket and Aunt Crys said . . ." Wini drifted off, not sure of her next thought.

"We called the Wildlife and Game Department," Crystal continued, reaching over and brushing her fingers against Wini's pink cheeks. "They came immediately and took the raccoon to the rehabilitation center until it was old enough to be released back into the woods. They told Wini she did a fantastic job of caring for it."

"And that's when I decided to be a veterinarian when I grow up," Wini said proudly, the long word sounding like two—vetra naryan.

"Well, we have a lot to talk about," Duncan said. "My sister is a veterinarian."

"Really?" Crystal and Wini asked in unison. "Jinx!" They both laughed, their faces turning bright red at their joke.

"You owe me a soda," Crystal declared, putting her arms around her grandniece and hugging her tight.

"Wini, Charlotte and I are going to check on Lovey, and you can stay and chat with Duncan for a bit. Is that okay with you?"

Wini nodded her head up and down. "Is that okay with you, Duncan Donut?"

"I would love nothing more than that."

Wini smiled, and Duncan couldn't help but now notice that prominent Kirk dimple in her chin.

Crystal and Charlotte rose from their chairs, Crystal placing a motherly kiss upon Wini's strawberry blonde head. "Remember your manners," she said, then turned her attention to Charlotte and small talk about Lovey, leaving Duncan Donut and his daughter to get to know one another.

CHAPTER 17

DUNCAN DONUT

"Do you want another s'more?" Wini asked, her eyes looking hopefully into Duncan's.

"I would. But only on the condition that you make it for me. I'm not very good at s'more making," he confessed.

Duncan watched Wini expertly construct the s'more, and he immediately thought that her concentration on building the perfect dessert reminded him of himself when he was in the midst of planning a project. It was all that existed for him, which of course led to a lot of other personal issues, but his focus, concentration, and scrutiny when he was designing consumed him. He could think of nothing more than seeing the task, from beginning to end, completed. At the time he met Isobel, he was in the thick of such a project. Although their relationship was a summer romance, at this moment, watching their daughter, he couldn't help but wonder if he'd paid more attention to Isobel than his work, if things might have been different. Would it have gone further? Would she have told him she was pregnant? Duncan would never know. He made decisions, for better or for worse. And now here he was, watching this young girl, the result of a summer love affair from eight years ago that he gave little attention to. But he knew one thing: He had a new life, and one person tempered his all-consuming need for professional perfection, and that was Charlotte. All the circumstances that guided his returning to Lobster Claw and to being in Elsie's Everything that stormy night in May, led him to her. He would never regret one step that brought him to this point in his life. Duncan knew, with Charlotte by his side, they could weather anything, including the fact that he had a child.

"Here you go," Wini proudly announced, handing Duncan the perfectly assembled s'more.

"This looks like it belongs in a cookbook," Duncan proclaimed, taking a bite into the perfect melding of melted marshmallow and milk chocolate squished in between two crisp graham crackers.

"Amazing!" he announced, taking another bite. "Wini, you've ruined me. I think I can only eat the s'mores you make." He took a paper napkin and wiped his mouth of the melted fusion now dripping on his chin.

Wini happily laughed. "Thank you. I've been making s'mores for a long time, so I'm pretty good at it. Let me know when you're ready for another."

"Don't worry, I will."

He wasn't used to conversing with children, but he didn't feel the awkwardness that he did when meeting colleagues' children at family business parties. Duncan saw that Wini was a very secure child, and she seemed comfortable meeting new people. *Here goes*, he thought, continuing the conversation with his little girl.

"What grade are you in at school?" *Sounds sort of silly, but a good starting point, I guess,* he thought, watching Wini pick up her half-eaten s'more.

"Third. I have a nice teacher, and we all like her a lot."

"Do you have any hobbies?" he asked.

Wini tilted her head as a look of perplexity crossed her rosy face. "What's a hobby?"

"Um, things you like to do outside school," Duncan replied, as he tried to think quickly of activities a child might enjoy. He knew what he liked to do at eight years old—build sandcastles, fish, climb the giant rocks at the beach.

"Oh!" Wini excitedly exclaimed, now understanding what Duncan meant. "Yes, I do. I like to read, and I play with Legos, and I like to bake and plant flowers. Me and Auntie Crys have a garden."

"That's amazing. You're a busy girl."

"I am. That's why Auntie Crys says I sleep good. I'm so busy all the time," she said with a laugh, biting into her s'mores.

"What's so funny?" Duncan asked, taking another bite of his. It was truly delicious.

"You have some marshmallow on your lip," she whispered, as she pointed to her own face to show him where it was. "You look a little like Santa Claus." Wini suddenly burst into a fit of giggles. Her left hand flew to her mouth to stifle them, but nothing was going to end them. Her already healthy pink face grew pinker, and her shoulders bobbed up and down in amusement.

Mom, Duncan thought, watching Wini, her eyes now closed because of her hard laughter. Duncan's mother was exactly like this when something particularly funny hit her. He, his father, and Ivy would also laugh because she looked like she was having the time of her life, as Wini was now. For a fleeting moment, Duncan was a little boy again, sitting across the table from his mother, who was laughing at one of his nonsensical childhood jokes. A sadness surged through Duncan as he watched Wini laugh, making him realize how much he missed his mother. At the same time however, he also felt a great sense of happiness, seeing that his mother still lived on in this child. His child. Duncan knew more than ever before he needed to be part of Wini's life, and he hoped that would be what she wanted, too.

Now was the time to find out. Duncan shifted in his chair, unsure how he should phrase his next question. *Just say it*, he thought. So he did. "Wini, your auntie Crystal told me you know I helped your mom's wish for a baby come true." He spoke slowly, carefully choosing his words. Despite her emotional intelligence, a gentle approach was needed, as Wini was a child and a motherless one at that.

"She did tell me about you," Wini simply said, picking up her spoon and scraping the remnants of her second s'mores and licking it like a lollipop. "And my mom said we would meet someday, too."

Duncan couldn't help but smile as Wini smiled, a bit of chocolate on her chin. Duncan refrained from wiping it away. *It's too adorable,* he thought.

"I was wondering, now that we have met, if you would like to meet again?"

"Hmm," Wini said, knitting her eyebrows in serious thought. She looked at Duncan, her eyes still bright, and her face pink, and for a moment he was swept up in a memory of him and Isobel, walking along Boston's Fan Pier, the wind kissing Isobel's face, and turning it the same shade of pink as Wini's was now.

"If you don't want to," Duncan began, "it's okay." The last thing he wanted to do was to pressure an eight-year-old into seeing a stranger, even though that stranger was her biological father.

"Of course I'd like to," Wini said. "But can I ask you something?"

Duncan felt heat rise into his cheeks and a nervous tension in his stomach, as he had no idea what she was about to ask him.

"Ask me anything," he said, trying to keep his composure.

"Can I call you Duncan Donut?"

Duncan felt a flood of relief run through him, and his body instantly relaxed at Wini's outburst of more giggles. She obviously thought his name was hilarious.

"Auntie Crys said I couldn't call you that unless I asked and got your permission."

"Permission granted," Duncan said to the amused child.

"Oh, here they come!" Wini announced, as Crystal and Charlotte returned from checking on Lovey.

"Auntie Crys," Wini said excitedly. "Duncan said I could call him Duncan Donut, and that he wants to see me again."

Duncan felt Crystal's eyes upon him as she sat down, and all he could do was nod his head and smile. Charlotte slipped back into her seat, and he smiled brightly at her, giving her a loving wink.

Crystal bobbed her head in agreement, and her smile instantly warmed Duncan as the foursome discussed plans on father and daughter's next steps.

CHAPTER 18

BITES, BLIZZARDS, AND MUD

"It's just beautiful, Tatiana. Just beautiful."

Charlotte admired the Christmas tree she and Tatiana decorated. They positioned it in the middle of the bay window of The Blue Hydrangea, looking out upon the Beach Block. Tatiana's collection of vintage ornaments and beautiful glass bulbs hung from the boughs like glittering jewels. Tiny white lights were threaded through the branches and gave the impression a million tiny stars were shining through the tree. From her bed near the door, Lovey's tail thumped happily in agreement.

"Everyone who sees it will say it's the most gorgeous tree they've ever seen!" Charlotte proclaimed, rearranging a small cluster of lights that bunched together on the tree's lower branches.

"Well, I certainly think it is," Tatiana said, smiling. She was gingerly replacing the unused ornaments back into their boxes.

"I can't believe it's Christmas time," Charlotte said as her hands adjusted the tiny lights on the tree.

"A lot has happened in the last six months." Tatiana walked over to Charlotte, who was now staring out of the bay window onto the Beach Block. She jumped slightly at Tatiana's caress on her right shoulder.

"It certainly has," Charlotte said, shaking her head, the trance now broken. She stuck her hands into a Rubbermaid container and pulled out a string of impossibly tangled lights. "Lobster Claw has been nothing short of incredible."

"Well, Lobster Claw is special. I think small towns get romanticized a lot, and people have moved here before and have moved right out after realizing its slow pace. I have to admit, I was a little worried about that with you when you first came up," said Tatiana.

Charlotte dropped the cluster of lights in surprise. "You never told me that." She turned to Tatiana. "Why did you think that?"

Charlotte watched as Tatiana gazed toward the top of the tree. An angel, its yellow hair matted upon its plastic face, was propped upon the top. In its small plastic hand was a candle, but it looked more like a cigarette to Charlotte, and she suppressed a giggle.

"Well, living in northern Maine is tough and is not as charming as movies make it out to be. The winters are long, albeit beautiful, and in the early spring, which you'll discover for yourself, the mud season can be, well, challenging. Those no-see-ums bite you without you knowing it until it's too late, and you're as itchy as a child with chickenpox. Not to mention the black flies."

"Oh, I am very much familiar with those. Remember all those bites I had on the back of my legs? I thought I had some kind of flesh-eating disease." Charlotte laughed, recalling the uncomfortable itchiness and sting of the bug bites.

"Well, the bites, the blizzards, and the mud have driven out even the heartiest of souls. But I thought you might be different, and I was right. I am so glad you're here." Tatiana smiled.

"Me, too. And don't you worry, no bug bites, blizzards, or mud is going to drive me away. I'm here to stay," Charlotte said, picking up the lights. She gave them a shake and the strand of lights magically fell from its tangled mass. "Voila! *Now* we will have the perfect tree."

"This is the last of the bulbs," Tatiana said, as she gently tucked away her precious ornaments. "How about some tea?"

"Absolutely," said Charlotte, trying to decide if the tree actually needed an extra set of lights.

Tatiana returned with the electric kettle and tea tray, poured boiling water over tea bags into the cups, then added a small dollop of golden honey to each cup. The simmering scent of the spiciness of the chai and the sweetness of the honey immediately relaxed Charlotte as she settled into the cushy wing chair.

"So, let's talk about Wini," Tatiana said. She took a seat opposite Charlotte in a matching chair.

"Wini," Charlotte whispered as she breathed in the scent of the chai. Charlotte did tell Tatiana about the girl, but she kept Tatiana's questions about Wini at arm's length. Unsure of her own feelings, Charlotte just did not want to delve into questions about this surprising discovery. This child was about to change everything regarding her relationship with Duncan. But it was weighing on her heavily, and under the comforting lights of Tatiana's Christmas tree, Charlotte decided it was time to open up.

"She's a little sweetheart. Wonderful manners. She seems very bright and perceptive, and extraordinarily well adjusted to everything that is happening to her," Charlotte said matter-of-factly, staring into her cup.

"Well, children are like that. I think they are much more resilient and accepting of life's circumstances than most adults can be. It sounds like she also has a wonderful grandaunt who is taking good care of her," Tatiana said.

Charlotte inhaled the warm and cozy scent of the cinnamon, cardamon, ginger, and cloves that was rising from her cup. She took a sip and sighed. "We've made plans for Wini and Crystal to visit the weekend before Christmas. We thought we'd go to the tree lighting and Santa parade."

"Oh, Charlotte, that's a wonderful idea. Wait until you see it yourself. It's beautiful, and Santa Claus arrives by boat," Tatiana said enthusiastically.

"I can't wait to see it," Charlotte smiled. She could see from Tatiana's thoughtful gaze that another question was coming.

"But you thought it would be you and Duncan this Christmas. And now this little surprise has changed things somewhat, hasn't she?"

Charlotte laughed at her friend's conjecture and the fact that Tatiana knew her so well. "She certainly has," she nodded in agreement. "She's an absolutely lovely child, and I liked her and Crystal very much. It's just such a bombshell, Tatiana. My relationship with Duncan is barely half a year old. We're navigating this later-in-life romance, and still learning about each other. I love and adore Duncan, and I'm sure we'll figure this out, but the only child I saw in our future was Ivy's. Not Duncan's daughter."

Lovey got up from her spot and crept over to her mistress, putting her yellow head gently in Charlotte's lap. Charlotte smiled down at her own girl and kissed the top of her silky head.

"You always know when Mom's a little worried, don't you, sweetie?" Charlotte lovingly petted Lovey. The plush yellow fur tickled her fingers, and she found such comfort in the softness of Lovey's coat. Charlotte and Lovey shared an incredible bond, and Lovey's intuition never ceased to amaze Charlotte. Somehow, this sweet dog could read all of Charlotte's moods, both good and bad.

Tatiana brought her chair next to Charlotte's and took hold of Charlotte's hands.

"There's nothing to worry about. Regardless of whether you and Duncan have been together for six months or for six years, you two have found each other, and you are committed to each other. There is no speedometer on love, Charlotte. Sometimes it's as slow as the proverbial tortoise and other times it has the horsepower of a Daytona 500 winner. We both know that."

Charlotte felt Tatiana's hold reassuringly tighten.

"Wini is a blessing. And I truly believe, if anything, she will make your relationship with Duncan deeper. He also can't do this without you. I have faith that Wini will have a profound impact on your relationship with Duncan, and in the very best way possible. Just take it slowly, roll with the punches—they'll be plenty," Tatiana laughed, "and I think you'll be in for an amazing surprise. Things happen for a reason. The reason may not be apparent now, but one day it will be clear."

Charlotte leaned over, unable to stop the sharply nipping tears in her eyes. She embraced Tatiana, who was not just a friend, but a confidante, a comforter, a soulmate. "What would I do without you?" Charlotte breathed the words as hot tears streamed down her cheeks. She was so grateful for Tatiana's wisdom, intuitiveness, and insight, all the invaluable qualities that made Tatiana Dulka the extraordinary person she was.

"I ask myself the same thing about you, my friend." Tatiana wiped the tears that had fallen on Charlotte's cheek with her thumb. "Think back to May and where you are now. All of this, you're coming here, meeting me, your relationship with Hamish, and he and I together again. This is no coincidence. It was all meant to be, and I am as grateful." Tatiana tenderly kissed Charlotte's forehead in a motherly fashion and took her face in her hands. "You're not alone, Charlotte. None of us are anymore. We are family, and we will always be here for one another. Calm seas or stormy skies, we'll weather it all together."

"We will. I promise," Charlotte said. "I feel so silly for crying. But you always know how to make me feel better." Lovey's loving lick on Charlotte's hand tickled, and she pulled Lovey close to her.

"And you, too, my sweet angel," she purred into Lovey's downy head. "You are so right." Charlotte sank back into her chair and drank her now lukewarm tea. "You just never know what life has in store for you, but if you're lucky enough to be surrounded by the people you love, well, it just makes it even more wonderful."

"And very interesting," Tatiana added with a smile.

"Interesting, for sure," Charlotte agreed, now feeling extremely optimistic about what the Christmas season had in store for her life, and all their lives, on Beach Rose Path.

CHAPTER 19

ARE YOU SURE?

Duncan stood on the bow of Callum's Pride, just returning from a ferrying job from Camden to collect Christmas supplies for Saturday's Lobster Claw Christmas Tree Lighting and Parade.

As he secured the boat's lines to the dock, Duncan's mind wandered to the discussion he and Charlotte had the previous night about Wini's upcoming visit.

Ever since they returned from Newport, Charlotte had been quiet about Wini, and last night was the first time they had an honest discussion about her.

"You haven't said too much about Wini. If you have any concerns . . ." Duncan had watched as Charlotte instantly shifted, her body now directly facing him, cutting off his words.

"How could I not have concerns? Our own relationship is still so new, and now we find out you have a child." She took a sip of her wine and continued. "I think I've been so quiet about it because it was surprising." She smiled, shrugging her shoulders. "And I'm sorry about that. I watched how you interacted with Wini at the restaurant, and that made me love you even more, if that's possible. But I'll be honest."

He'd heard the change in Charlotte's tone; her voice had become whisper-like, almost as if she was hesitant to speak.

"I was afraid of the impact I thought this would have on our relationship. But I'm not any longer."

"Afraid?" Duncan asked, his heart racing anxiously for what she was about to say. Then Charlotte had smiled that reassuring smile, and Duncan's heart had instantly slowed down.

"Yes, afraid. Tatiana and I had a long talk about it, and as she always does, she made me realize that having Wini in our lives will only strengthen us. And I absolutely believe that. I've been quiet because I know it's a lot for you to take in as well, but we can tackle it together."

Snapping him back to the present and instantly interrupting his thoughts of the previous evening, someone yelled his name. "Hey, Duncan!"

He glanced at the dock and saw Elsie McEverett waving her arms frantically, as if she was in distress.

"Elsie! Everything okay?" Duncan quickly secured the lines, hopped off the boat, and jogged toward her.

"Oh, yeah, everything's fine. It's just about the Christmas tree . . ."

Duncan smiled at the frantic woman. Strands of hair were loosely and wildly flying about her round and full pink face, despite her usual practice of tying her hair in a neat and tight bun at the back of her head. She pursed her lips, and Duncan knew from this gesture he had seen many times before, she needed him to make 'a special delivery.' He felt this request was about to burst from those pursed lips. "What about the tree?" Duncan asked innocently, fully aware that she needed something.

"Well, those special lights we use? The store in Camden forgot to put a couple of cases on your last run," she stammered.

Duncan laughed, laying a reassuring hand on Elsie's shoulder. If it were not for Elsie's Everything, her general store, he may never have met Charlotte; and he knew, no matter what the request, he would take care of her. He suspected she knew that as well.

"Yeah, the lobstermen just finished constructing it," Elsie said.

"Constructing a tree?" Duncan, as happened often when conversing with Elsie, did not know where the conversation might lead to.

"Well, I know it's been a while since you spent a Christmas here, and things have changed. For the better, of course." A dazzling smile of delight now beamed on Elsie's face, and Duncan couldn't help but smile back at her mischievousness. She then playfully punched him in the shoulder.

"You get those lights, bring them to me, and I promise you a tree the likes that you have never seen before." She then winked at him. "Okay?"

Duncan wrapped his arms around the woman who was responsible for all the happiness he had in his life now and tenderly kissed her forehead. "Whatever you need, Elsie. Just text me all the details, and I'll have those lights for you tomorrow by noon. That work?"

"Oh, wonderful. You'll have one of your favorite double cheeseburgers waiting for you when you get back, and I'll even splurge for extra mushrooms!"

"You're the best, Elsie. Just don't forget to text me."

"I will when I get back to the Everything. Thanks, love!"

Duncan watched Elsie happily trot to her minivan and speed off toward Sand Dollar Drive back to what everyone in Lobster Claw referred to as the Everything. And it certainly had everything —even the woman who changed his life in all the best ways imaginable.

"That was fast," Duncan said, hearing the ping of his cellphone, believing the message was sent by Elsie. But he saw it was actually from Crystal.

We have our train reservations. We leave Providence at seven in the morning and will arrive in Brunswick at two on Saturday.

Perfect. I'll be at the Brunswick train station well before then. Looking forward to seeing you both, Duncan immediately texted back.

An emoji with a smiley face appeared from Crystal, and he put the phone in his jacket pocket.

Arrangements had been made for Crystal and Wini to come up to Lobster Claw for the tree lighting and Christmas parade on December 21. December 20 was Wini's last day of school before the long and luxurious Christmas break. Duncan and Charlotte thought it would be the perfect opportunity for them to visit Lobster Claw in all its Christmas beauty. Crystal made reservations at a new B&B that opened this past summer on the outskirts of Lobster Claw, about five miles south down Sand Dollar Drive. Duncan and Crystal agreed to take things slowly, and if this trip proved successful, then they would talk about the possibility of future visits.

"One thing at a time," Duncan said, as he gave the lines an extra pull to make sure they were secure until morning. Now he was off for a visit with Ivy, and of course, looking forward to a relaxing evening with Charlotte.

CHAPTER 20

ALL SET

"I'm all set, Auntie Crys," Wini announced, marching into the living room with her Fancy Firefly duffle bag, an early Christmas present from Crystal.

Crystal believed that giving Wini a surprise gift would make their trip more exciting and enjoyable. Crystal was a huge fan of the pretty and popular totes and bags, and always stocked up when a sale announcement arrived in her email. That way, she always had a special gift prepared, and this was one of those times.

She placed her own bag next to Wini's with a plop. She exclaimed, "Wonderful! Me too. Let's get to bed early tonight. I made a reservation with a car service to pick us up in the morning at seven sharp to drive us to Providence, where we get on the train at nine. We should be in Maine by two. Sound good?"

"Sounds great, Auntie Crys!" Wini glanced at the illuminated clock on the stove. The green numbers announced it was seven-thirty. "I'm going to bed now so I can get up nice and early. It's going to be so much fun. I hope I can sleep."

Crystal laughed at her grandniece's genuine excitement. She knew Wini was looking forward to seeing Duncan and Charlotte, and watching the parade and tree lighting ceremony. And, of course, Lovey was all she talked about.

"Get into bed and I'll read you a story."

Wini shook her head. "No stories tonight. I'm going straight to sleep."

"Good idea," Crystal agreed. She followed Wini into her bedroom, tucked her in, and kissed her goodnight. She turned on the reindeer night-light that was plugged in near her bedroom door and softly closed the door.

CHAPTER 21

IN THIS TOGETHER

"Okay, sweetie. Calm down," Charlotte said, laughing as her ever-enthusiastic pup let her know with her furious tail wagging that Duncan was here. She opened her front door and saw Duncan get out of his truck. He locked the truck but remained rooted in the driveway. He rubbed his large hands together as if he needed to warm them, and Charlotte smiled at this nervous quirk of his. As confident as he liked to appear, she knew from his hand rubbing that he was anxious, and it simply enchanted her.

"Good morning," he said, walking up to her and kissing her as if he hadn't seen her in days instead of hours.

She couldn't resist reaching into his perfectly coiffed hair and messing it up a bit. "There. That's better. That's the Duncan I know and love." She laughed, leaning up to kiss him on the cheek. He wrapped his arms tightly around her body, and she felt a feathery soft kiss on her cheek. "Don't try too hard," she said, as they headed inside. "They already like you. A lot."

"I don't know why I'm so nervous," Duncan said as he rubbed his hands. "We've already faced the hard part, and that went well."

Charlotte looked into his hazel eyes and thought she detected a shadow of doubt—some kind of uneasiness that seemed to trouble him. She reached out her hand to him. "Come on, let's take a quick walk on the beach. It will relax Lovey before the ride, and we can talk. Something's bothering you, and I want to know what it is."

For the past six months, whenever Charlotte was full of doubts herself, and she certainly was, she and Lovey always walked along the craggy shoreline. She found the ocean walks healing and restorative, both physically and mentally, and after even a short walk, Charlotte felt as if she could tackle the world. Once she and Duncan became closer, they enjoyed these walks together, talking about their lives, their pasts, and their future. Throughout their walks, they never broached the subject of children, as they had already closed that chapter in their lives, both being in their fifties. However, with Ivy's pregnancy news, a new chapter was beginning. Duncan was about to become an uncle, and Charlotte an honorary aunt. Everyone on the Beach Block was looking forward to the newest Lobster Claw citizen. And now Wini was about to enter the scene.

Duncan's daughter. The road to their future had just taken a sharp exit, and Charlotte had confessed her fears and doubts to Tatiana. Duncan had been quiet about it lately, but Charlotte knew something was bothering him. She was determined to find out what it was, especially before the big weekend visit.

The crash of the surf lured Lovey, and she ran directly to the shore, frolicking in the whitecaps, jumping and pawing the small waves, prancing in the ocean's froth. She was such an obedient dog and never strayed out of Charlotte's sight. If Lovey thought she had gone too far, she always turned to make sure Charlotte was trailing behind her.

The wind was cold and bracing. Pushed by the wind, the puffy white clouds gave the sky a clear and serene appearance. The forecast called for clear blue skies and bright starry nights, with a full moon on the rise. Not a flake of snow was predicted. It wouldn't be a white Christmas, but Charlotte didn't mind. She loved the cold, and she knew the snow would come.

"I know it's been a lot," Charlotte began, snuggling into the buttery softness of Duncan's leather bomber jacket as he wrapped his arms around her shoulder, "but you've been quiet about what's happened. I know this is life changing, but you can talk to me."

Duncan's one-armed embrace tightened around her shoulder; she knew he heard her and that his feelings were safe with her.

"I'm sorry," he said, planting a kiss on top of her wavy and windblown hair. "It's a part of me you haven't experienced because you haven't had to. I have a tendency to close down when something beyond my control happens. And Wini is certainly beyond my control. I almost didn't have time to think or process the situation before we went to Newport. I fully committed to meeting her and didn't even consider the consequences. She is my daughter and my responsibility, and I was going to face this head on. But since we've been back, and I've actually had time to think about it, I think maybe I acted too quickly. It was different in Newport—we drove there, met, and we came back home. Now she's coming here —to our home. I know you're welcoming her with open arms, but I know I've been closemouthed on this and I should have opened up more. But, like I said, that's how I can get."

Their walking slowed as they approached the ragged rock formation that led to Sea Star Lighthouse, Charlotte's stalwart beacon of hope, of light. She relied on Sea Star Lighthouse through her darkest times when she first arrived in Lobster Claw. Its ever present beam that glowed every evening assured her it was not only lighting the way for ships through the darkness of night, but for her life as well. She believed the lighthouse's unwavering light was a source of strength, guiding her through her own stormy seas. She knew she had to be Duncan's guiding star through his turbulence. She led him to their favorite spot—a smoothed-out landing among the rugged rocks on which they loved to sit and watch the sun go down. They held each other as they looked at the waves crash over the rocks, and Charlotte felt that they, and Lovey, were the only ones who existed.

She lovingly squeezed his hand. "Sometimes, you can't think about how to proceed in certain situations. If I gave myself time to think about moving here, I might not be here. I just did it. I didn't have time to think."

"You did the right thing. And this weekend is the right thing. Their visit is coming at a perfect time. There's so much to do here, they will stay entertained every minute. Remember, you are not alone. We're in this together."

The caress of Duncan's calloused hands on her face sent shivers throughout her body. She looked into his eyes, and the shadow of doubt that was there earlier had disappeared; the love and trust had returned.

"I love you so much, Charlotte," Duncan whispered as he kissed her desperately, as if this kiss was all he needed to face whatever was to come their way. She relished his kisses, but this kiss was especially meaningful. She felt the love and trust she had just seen in his eyes now in the press of his lips. The kiss was interrupted by Lovey's wild barking, and Charlotte turned to see Lovey barking at a beachcomber scanning the sand for treasures along the shore. Lovey had signaled they were no longer alone, and that it was time to go.

"Good girl," Duncan said, laughing.

They got up, and Charlotte followed Duncan, his hand tightly ensconced around hers. The two of them, with Lovey close behind, made their way down the rocky ledge and headed back to Beach Rose Path. Charlotte bundled in close to him, now very much looking forward to the next few days.

Chapter 22

Welcome to Lobster Claw

Charlotte watched Duncan steer his truck into the open spot in the parking lot at the Brunswick train station. Lovey sat in the back seat, looking about expectantly as if she knew her new friends would be arriving. They hopped out of the truck and Duncan grabbed his foam coffee cup.

He glanced at his watch. "Few more minutes," he said.

Charlotte saw him wince as he took a sip from his cup. "Cold?" she laughed?

"Like ice," he said, his face still distorted in disgust.

The loud clanging of train bells alerted them that the Providence train was now pulling into Brunswick Station.

Charlotte felt a slight tinge of apprehension rise in her stomach, a small knot tightening as the train bells loudly rang. She then noticed Duncan was rocking back and forth on the heels of his feet, another nervous habit when something weighed heavily on his mind. Charlotte realized he was just as nervous, and she gave him a reassuring touch, grasping his hand and putting it to her lips.

"This will be fun. Don't put too much pressure on yourself.

Remember, they're probably nervous as well." She breathed deeply and the tension in her stomach subsided, as did Duncan's heel rocking.

"Let's do this," he said with a smile.

Charlotte opened the truck's back door and put Lovey on her lead. Lovey happily pounced onto the ground and Charlotte slipped her a small treat.

They walked toward the platform and immediately saw Wini, dressed in jeans and a green puffer coat. Her pretty strawberry blonde hair was loose and cascaded down her shoulders, bouncing with the girl's every step. She waved wildly at seeing Lovey, and Charlotte could see a bright smile light up Wini's wind-kissed face. Crystal walked closely behind, and Charlotte noticed the Fancy Firefly duffle bags on their shoulders. It reminded her of her time at Castle Loch, as that was one of her favorite women's clothing brands she sold in the pro shop.

"Here," Charlotte whispered to Duncan. "Take Lovey and meet her. I'll wait here by the truck."

Duncan smiled and kissed Charlotte's cheek. "Let's go, Lovey," he said, and together they walked up the stairs to the train platform.

"Hi, Duncan Donut!" Wini enthusiastically shouted. She ran toward them and instantly kneeled to hug Lovey, who greeted Wini with a multitude of happy and sloppy kisses, making Wini laugh enthusiastically.

"It's good to see you again, Duncan," Crystal said, giving him a warm embrace.

"Welcome to Maine," he said. "We're all set for you—truck's all cleaned out and plenty of room for your bags." He pointed to where Charlotte was standing. She smiled and waved.

"Hi, Charlotte!" Wini called.

Charlotte noticed Wini was holding Lovey's leash. *Thank God for Lovey*, she thought as her precious dog was the perfect icebreaker once again, making Wini feel comfortable in a brand new environment. Charlotte watched as Duncan took their bags and the foursome walked toward the truck.

"Well, hello, Wini. It's so nice to see you again." Charlotte instinctively bent down and hugged her. Her small arms wrapped around Charlotte's neck and the clean scent of lemon shampoo infiltrated Charlotte's nostrils.

"I'm glad you brought Lovey," Wini said, petting the dog on her head.

"She couldn't wait to see you. Are you ready for a fun weekend?" Charlotte thought talking about all the Lobster Claw Christmas activities would be another way to ease the pressure off the visit as well.

"I know I am," Crystal said, extending her arms and Charlotte gratefully returned the woman's friendly hug. "Nice to see you, Charlotte, and nice to see you too, Lovey," Crystal said, smiling at the obedient dog, who was patiently sitting and waiting to get into the truck

Duncan put the duffels into the bed, which he had covered for the winter. Since the truck could fit five, everyone had plenty of room in the cab, with Crystal behind Duncan, Wini behind Charlotte, and Lovey sitting in the middle.

"We'll get you settled into the B&B first," Charlotte explained. "It's new and seems so charming. I think you'll both like it."

Duncan started the truck and pulled out onto the highway that would take them back to Lobster Claw. Charlotte, Crystal, and Wini happily chatted about all the Christmas activities that were planned for the weekend, as well as their shared love for the Fancy Firefly.

The conversation flowed effortlessly, like they were old friends who hadn't seen each other in ages.

They spoke mainly about the new B&B and the festivities, with Duncan contributing information about a bridge they were crossing—its age and construction—which caused the women to burst into laughter.

"Forgive me, ladies, but whenever I see an architectural wonder, I ramble uncontrollably." His laugh was laid back, and Charlotte smiled, knowing he was feeling comfortable, especially with this architectural blathering.

"Oh, look!" Wini pointed towards the windshield.

"That is exactly what I saw when I first came to Lobster Claw," Charlotte said, turning around and speaking to Wini. A wooden sign in the shape of a huge red lobster proclaiming *Welcome to Lobster Claw, Maine. Get caught in our claws and stay a while* came into view.

"It's so funny," Wini said, laughing.

"I thought the same thing," Charlotte agreed, remembering the first time she entered Lobster Claw and drove down Sand Dollar Drive to Beach Rose Path.

"And here we are," Duncan announced. He pulled into the drive of a beautifully decorated two-story home. At each end of the porch, pine trees were adorned with strings of tiny white lights. A life-sized Santa stood in greeting, and a magnificent evergreen wreath hung on the door front. The large silver bell that was tied to the wreath jingled as Duncan opened the elegantly decorated door.

"This is absolutely lovely," Crystal said as she followed Duncan into a beautifully decorated foyer. The highly polished mahogany floors shone from the sunlight streaming in from the windows. To their right, a white-painted staircase was decorated with evergreen garlands and tiny white lights, mirroring the porch's festive trees.

As they entered the cozy living room, the crackling sounds of the welcoming fire in the fireplace filled the air. The fireplace was decorated with brilliant red poinsettias on either side, and the mantel was adorned with sprigs of holly, candles, and stockings.

The Christmas tree, which touched the ceiling, stood in a corner next to the fireplace. Cranberry garlands and dried oranges were strung expertly on each bough. Rustic, wooden ornaments in the shapes of bunnies, brown bears, and reindeer dangled from the boughs, which were prettily illuminated by colored lights.

Charlotte noticed a bell on the fireplace mantel. She shrugged her shoulders at the little group and picked it up and shook it, which created a pretty seasonal tinkling sound.

"Coming!" a voice from the back of the house called. A woman magically appeared from behind the Christmas tree. Charlotte took a closer look and saw an entryway that was concealed behind the mammoth tree.

"Charlotte and Duncan! So nice to see you again. These must be your guests."

Chloe Branch extended her slender hand. Her short nails were painted a bright Christmas red. She was a tall woman, and Charlotte had heard someone in her store mention that Chloe stood over six feet tall. Her short hair was salt and peppered and hanging from her earlobes were bell-shaped earrings, which tinkled softly with every movement of her head. She wore jeans and a black turtle-neck sweater, covered by a festive red apron.

"Chloe, this is Crystal and Wini Frost. All the way from Newport for all the Lobster Claw festivities this weekend," Duncan said, and made the introductions.

"Welcome. I'm a bit of a newcomer myself. Retired from nursing in Portland, and now living my dream running this bed and breakfast. And it's been quite exciting. Can I get you anything —coffee, tea, hot cocoa?" she asked, glancing Wini's way.

"Coffee would be wonderful," Crystal said, then turned to Wini. "And I think Wini would love a cup of cocoa."

"I would, thank you, Aunt Crys and Mrs. . . ." Wini stopped, evidently forgetting Chloe's last name.

"No formalities, Wini. Just call me Chloe," she said, nodding towards Duncan and Charlotte. "Can I get you something?"

"We're all set, but thanks," Duncan answered. "Charlotte and I wanted to give Crystal and Wini some time to settle in. We'll be back around six-thirty. The tree lighting is at seven, and the parade is right after that."

"Sounds great, Duncan Donut," Wini said, smiling up at Duncan.

Charlotte saw Duncan's face light up at Wini's term of endearment.

"Go have your cocoa," Charlotte said, bending down to Wini's eye level. "I'll bring Lovey home for her nap before tonight. We'll see you in a few hours."

Wini smiled. "Thank you, Charlotte," she said. Suddenly, Wini's arms wrapped around Charlotte's neck. The sweet and caring gesture deeply moved Charlotte, bringing tears to her eyes. She barely knew this little girl, yet Wini felt comfortable enough to hug her. It was a Christmas present in itself.

"I can't wait for tonight," whispered Charlotte. She rose and took Lovey back outside before her tears were evident to everyone. Wini's thoughtful hug caught her off guard, and Charlotte hadn't realized how this could evoke such emotion. It reminded her of when Landon first handed her Peppercorn on that Christmas Eve long ago. The innate maternal feeling of wanting to love and protect someone rushed over her. This happened again when she discovered the homeless dog with her only puppy in the basement at Beach Rose Path. And now Wini held the same emotional power over her.

The cold December air rushed through Charlotte, drying her eyes of tears.

"You okay?" Duncan asked, putting his hand on her shoulder as he joined her on the porch.

Charlotte's emotions were now in check, the chilly breeze felt invigorating, and the feel of Christmas was in the air.

"I am," she said, gently covering Duncan's hand with her own. "I just didn't expect Wini to hug me. And suddenly, all these emotions overpowered me. Duncan, she amazes me. This child, whom we barely know, has been through so much, yet she is incredibly accepting and loving towards people she has just met. She's truly special, Duncan," Charlotte said, gazing into his hazel eyes.

"You're special," he whispered, giving Charlotte a sweet kiss on her forehead.

She hugged him tightly and then they headed back to the truck.

"I'm going to open the shop for a bit. Tatiana texted and said a busload of tourists has descended on the Beach Block. It won't hurt to make some extra Christmas bucks," she said, ensuring Lovey was settled into her seat.

"Nice," Duncan said. "And you know what I need to get ready for," he smiled.

"Actually, I don't, since you haven't elaborated one bit on what you are up to, Mr. Kirk," she said, chuckling, the sound of her laughter filling the truck. "All you've been saying is that 'I'm working on something special.'"

With a click, she fastened her seatbelt, feeling the familiar sense of security as Duncan maneuvered the truck along Sand Dollar Drive. Although it was cold, Charlotte rolled the windows down to catch the scent of salty sea air mixing with the distant sound of crashing waves. A cold blast assailed her, and she put the window right back up.

"It's the season of surprises." Duncan kept his gaze on the road.

Charlotte sighed and rolled her eyes. She knew he was planning something, but did not know what, and she didn't want to know. If it was a surprise from Duncan Kirk, she knew it would be amazing.

Charlotte's phone pinged her out of her romantic thoughts and she reached for it in her coat pocket.

"Must be Tatiana," she said, thinking Tatiana was providing tourist updates.

"Oh, no," Charlotte said.

"What's wrong?" Duncan asked, turning to look at her.

"There's been an accident. We need to get back to the B&B." She felt the swift swerve of the truck as Duncan immediately responded to her urgent tone, making a U-turn on Sand Dollar Drive and racing back to Chloe's.

CHAPTER 23

THOSE SLIPPERS

"I'm really okay. I truly am. It's all my fault as it is, anyway." Crystal was lying on the couch in the living room at the B&B. Chloe skillfully raised Crystal's leg to the perfect angle and propped her foot up on a pile of pillows with a bag of ice on her swollen ankle as Duncan and Charlotte walked through the door.

"What on Earth happened?" Duncan asked, dashing into the B&B.

Wini was sitting on the ottoman, facing her grandaunt and shaking her head.

"It was those slippers, Auntie Crys. Mommy always said after the last time you fell in them not to wear them. Remember?"

Charlotte could see the consternation on Wini's face—her eyebrows knitted and her mouth a firm, straight line. She couldn't help but smile at the girl's reprimand.

Crystal took Wini's hand in hers. "You're right. Your mother told me, and I didn't listen, and I should have."

"What happened?" Charlotte asked. She didn't have to be a medical professional to see that Crystal's ankle looked terrible. It was purple and twice its normal size.

"Oh, I wanted to get out of my boots, so as soon as you two

left, I took my bag upstairs and put these on," she said, pointing to an ancient-looking pair of light blue slip-on slippers that were on the floor by the couch.

"They're really old," Wini added. "Mommy always said there were no tracks—" Wini stopped, appearing to not be able to think of how to describe the slippers.

Crystal smiled at her grandniece. "Your mother was right. There's no traction on these slippers," she said, now looking up at Duncan and Charlotte. "They were my mother's. I gave them to her on her last Christmas, and, well, I couldn't bear to part with them. I know I have to be extra careful when I wear them, but as I was coming down the stairs, I slipped and ended up here," she said, throwing her hands up in defeat. "I'm just grateful I landed on the couch of a retired nurse!"

"That makes two of us," Chloe said stoically, readjusting the pillows beneath Crystal's ankle. "I don't think it's broken, but it's a good idea to get an x-ray."

Crystal laughed and waved away the suggestion, as if shooing away an annoying insect. "Oh, heavens no! This is nothing. I've had worse."

"She has," Wini chimed in. "Last time this happened, it was way purpler and bigger. Right, Auntie Crys?"

Crystal nodded in agreement. "Right, sweetie," she said. A flush of embarrassment colored her cheeks. She shook her head, and her eyes were downcast.

"I'll get you some acetaminophen for the swelling and pain. Also, I'll switch your order from coffee to tea. You should relax and stay where you are." Chloe headed to the kitchen to get what she needed to take care of her new patient.

Crystal's eyes welled with tears, and she forcefully shrugged off the fleece throw Chloe draped over her legs. She tried to stand up, but her face contorted in a grimace of pain. She slowly laid back down on the sofa. "Oh, I am sorry," Crystal said, as tears streamed down her cheeks.

Charlotte bent by her side, placing a reassuring hand on the woman's shoulders.

"There's no need to apologize," she said, her voice whisper-like and soothing. "Accidents happen, and we should be grateful it wasn't worse, right?" She smiled, hoping that her words would comfort Crystal. Crystal wiped away her tears with trembling hands.

"It's okay, Auntie Crys. I can stay here with you. I don't mind at all. It's really pretty in here, anyway." Wini knelt next to her grandaunt and kissed Crystal's wet cheek.

"Wini, you can still come with Charlotte, Lovey, and me, if you'd like." Duncan's voice was quiet yet hopeful.

Wini looked back at Duncan as a sweet smile lengthened across her face.

"Wini, go with them. I'll be fine here, waiting for you. When you come back, tell me all about it," Crystal said. A brave smile formed on her face as she reached out her arms to hug her grandniece.

Chloe returned with a mug of steaming tea and Crystal's medicine. "Your aunt is going to be just fine, sweetie," she said.

"Duncan and I were on our way back to my shop. If it's okay with your aunt, you can come with us now. You can see my shop, and we can take Lovey for a quick walk on the beach." Charlotte then turned to Crystal. "I'm happy to FaceTime you as soon as we get to the shop and from the parade, if you'd like." Charlotte knew it was important for Crystal to know that Wini would be in excellent hands. "This way you can rest and not worry."

"I cannot thank you enough, Charlotte. And Duncan. Oh, and Lovey." Crystal outstretched her arms toward her grandniece, who melted into them.

"Be on your best behavior, sweetie," Crystal whispered. "And most importantly, do not worry about me, and have fun. Okay?"

Wini buried her face in the nape of her grandaunt's neck and hugged her tightly.

"I promise, Auntie Crys." She then turned to Charlotte. "Is it okay to take lots of pictures to send to Auntie Crys?" Wini's concern for her grandaunt touched Charlotte.

"We can take as many as you want," Charlotte said with a smile.

"I left my coat in the kitchen. I'll go get it." Wini skipped from the living room into the kitchen.

"Thank you so much," Crystal said, looking back toward the kitchen and speaking in hushed tones. "I just want to keep her as busy as possible, as, well, you know, it will be her—"

"Don't even think about it," Duncan interrupted, stopping Crystal from having to say, "first Christmas without her mom."

Charlotte knew full well how agonizing those "firsts" were, especially during the holidays. The plan was to keep Wini occupied and happy, which would hopefully ease the pain of not only missing Isobel, but now Crystal's predicament as well.

"I'm ready," Wini announced as she zipped her green puffer coat.

"Oh, don't forget a hat and gloves," Crystal reminded her. "It's cold out there."

"Okay. Be right back." Wini ran up the stairs to their room and was back in a flash with a hat and mittens.

"While you all are gone, I'm going to move you two downstairs into the suite in the back next to the kitchen. It will make things easier for you, Crystal," Chloe said. "You all have a great time tonight. Don't hurry back." Chloe padded into the kitchen to ready the suite.

"Bye, Auntie Crys," Wini said, leaning in to hug her grandaunt goodbye. "I love you and I promise to be good."

Crystal hugged her grandniece tightly. "Oh, I know you will. Have a good time, and I can't wait to hear all about it."

"We promise to text lots of pictures," Charlotte said, reaching her hand toward Wini.

"Ready for a Lobster Claw Christmas?" Duncan asked as he heralded Charlotte and Wini outside.

"I know I am," said Charlotte. "It's my first Lobster Claw Christmas too, Wini. I'm glad we can experience it together."

Wini beamed, her pretty smile lighting up her face. "Me too," she said.

"Here we go," Duncan said as he ushered them into the truck. Lovey's tail banged in happiness as she saw them get in, and they set off for what Charlotte hoped would be an unforgettable Lobster Claw Christmas adventure.

CHAPTER 24

WHAT A BEAUTIFUL FAMILY

Lying on her bed, Crystal was in agony as searing jolts of pain pulsated in her ankle with excruciating throbs. That would have been easy enough to handle with pain medication, but there was another pain she was feeling that no painkiller in the world would dull, and that was the potential prospect of losing Wini. She knew she was being silly and that it was the discomfort and exhaustion she was feeling, but watching Wini, Charlotte, and Duncan leave the B&B, she didn't see two adults and a child walk out the front door—for a brief moment, she saw a family off to enjoy an evening of Christmas festivities.

She took a deep breath and looked around the suite. It was spacious and cozy, dominated by a king-sized bed. Strands of colored lights hung over the massive wooden headboard, while a small Christmas tree stood in a corner, adorned with red and gold ornaments and illuminated with twinkly bright white lights. The softness of the flannel sheets caressed her sore and tired body, and Crystal felt she was lying upon a bed of feathers. Several propped up extra-large pillows elevated her engorged foot. She disliked taking any painkillers at all, but she knew she needed them for the swelling, so she relented and took them. She thought the pain medication was also impacting her mental state, leading to visions of Wini being swept away by her biological father, his attractive and compassionate companion, along with their perfect dog.

Crystal, at sixty-five, had never married, and had spent her adult life in the skies as a flight attendant. She loved the adventure, never being someone to stay in one place for too long. But when a pregnant Isobel returned to Rhode Island, she became a surrogate mother to her and then eventually to Wini. Making a promise to Isobel, she assured her she would take care of Wini. She also promised, much to her consternation, that if Duncan wanted to meet Wini, Crystal would ensure that would happen. Even though she didn't agree with Isobel on this one issue, she promised.

Now, here they were, in a picturesque Maine town, far from Newport. Crystal's heart longed for home, to be with Wini there and enjoy their Christmas together. Behind her closed eyes, images of Wini, Duncan, and Charlotte played like a movie—a movie of them gazing upon a huge pine tree the size of the Empire State Building being lit, the magic of a parade of elves, reindeer, and Santa Claus marching through the streets of Lobster Claw, with drums, horns, and all the holiday charms of a Christmas parade. She could see their radiant smiles as Santa Claus rode in a beautiful sleigh straight from the North Pole, and the magic and the wonder that he would bring to everyone who believed.

Crystal's head now ached as intensely as her ankle as her mind played out scenes of Wini happily perched on Duncan's shoulders, watching the dancing elves and Santa's friendly wave. Wini walking hand in hand with Charlotte and Duncan down the street, with Lovey faithfully following behind, all on the hunt for hot chocolate.

What a beautiful family. Crystal could hear the whispers of the spectators as the three of them walked by, happy and oblivious to anything or anyone else except each other.

A strong protective feeling for her little family suddenly jolted Crystal from near sleep. A wave of anxious fear washed over her as her heartbeat quickened and sweat bathed her forehead. Despite liking Duncan and Charlotte, the potential loss of Wini overwhelmed her, causing tears and an unrestful night.

Right before she fell asleep, Crystal realized how crucial it was to her to protect her little family, and a plan started forming in her spent and weary mind.

CHAPTER 25

NO ORDINARY MAN

Charlotte tucked her hands inside of her jacket pockets. Her hands were cold in spite of her gloves, thanks to the frigid night air.

"Wini! I am so pleased to meet you. I have heard so much about you." Tatiana joined them at the tree lighting area at the end of the dock, where the boats were secured for the winter.

"Nice to meet you, too," Wini said, smiling. She then turned her attention to Duncan. "I don't see a Christmas tree here, Duncan Donut."

Tatiana chuckled at Duncan's adorable nickname and then looked back at Wini. "It's a special type of tree, Wini. You'll only see this in Lobster Claw. It's been a tradition here for over seventy-five years, even before I was born." Tatiana smiled and winked at the little girl. "I think you'll really like it."

"Okay, everyone! We are just about ready to light the tree!" Harry, owner of Harry's Surf and Turf was the emcee for the evening's events. This honor had been bestowed upon Harry for the last ten years—he was actually the only one who ever wanted to do it—and every year his showmanship grew with his role.

"Here we go, Wini," Tatiana whispered as the large crowd gathered in the frosty night.

"Now, just a brief history before we light this beauty. We like to do things a little differently in Lobster Claw, and almost one hundred years ago, Lobster Claw's founder, Efram McEverett, wanted to celebrate Christmas by paying homage to what this town began as and still is—a fishing village. This Lobster Claw tradition started humbly, and over the decades, it became more elaborate, and we think, this year, it's the best. So, without further ado, ladies and gentlemen, children of all ages, let me present to you this year's Lobster Claw Christmas Tree! Everyone count down with me, and I want everyone to look up at Elsie McEverett." Harry enthusiastically waved to Elsie, who was standing inside the bucket of a work crane. She was at the top of the tree on the cold December night. A huge tarp covered a triangular shape, as the temporary fence that had fiercely guarded the tree was dismantled earlier in the day,

"You ready up there, Elsie?" Harry asked through his blow horn.

"Ready as I'll ever be, Harry! Start the countdown already! It's freezing!" Elsie commanded.

Everyone laughed and chanted, "Countdown, countdown!"

"Okay, everyone! 5. 4. 3. 2. 1. Merry Christmas!"

Elsie pulled on a wire, and down came the tarp. The sound of surprised gasps filled the air.

Before the crowd stood a massive "tree" made entirely of lobster traps and buoys, reaching a height of at least thirty feet. Thousands of multicolored lights illuminated it. Atop the highest crate sat a brightly lit lobster, holding a shining gold star in its claws.

Collective gasps of pure amazement emitted from the crowd, then a hush descended as everyone gazed up at the magnificent and unique tree.

"Gets better every year, Harry!" a man acknowledged from the crowd.

"Okay, everyone!" Harry began again as the bucket truck lowered Elsie, and she hopped out to join Harry. "Our tree this year has a special touch. Unlike previous years, you'll actually have the chance to step inside the Christmas tree." Harry indicated the doorway, constructed from old door frames and topped with a rustic sign reading "Lobster Claw Christmas Tree."

"Now, this will be open until midnight tonight, so you'll all have plenty of time to see the inside. For those who would like to visit now, we ask that you form a line right behind Elsie, who will be our Christmas tree concierge for the season. Elsie, it's all yours." Harry jogged away from the tree and towards the other end of the dock.

"Can we go inside now?" Wini asked.

Duncan kneeled before Wini, taking her hands in hers. "I have a very important Christmas favor to do for someone, so you, Charlotte, Tatiana, and Lovey can go in now, and we can go in again when I come back. Is that okay with you?"

"You mean we can go inside again, Duncan Donut?" Wini's face was as bright as the lights on the Christmas tree, and she wrapped her arms around Duncan's neck.

"I take that as a yes?" Duncan asked, his own brilliant smile flashing across his ruddy and handsome face.

Father and daughter were still strangers, but they shared a biological connection. Charlotte watched the sweet exchange and marveled at their faces—so extraordinarily similar—the curve of their lips when they smiled, the dimpled chin, the way their eyes brightened when they were happy. She knew, of course, there was no doubt a lot of Isobel in Wini, but as people would say when they saw a new baby or a child, "she's all Kirk."

Charlotte felt a hand on her shoulder and turned to see Tatiana's smiling face.

"Elsie is signaling for us," she said to Charlotte, nodding toward Elsie, who was wildly waving at the little group.

Charlotte gently laid her hand over Tatiana's, providing reassurance, knowing Tatiana was also watching the affectionate scene between father and daughter. However, Charlotte and Tatiana knew Duncan had important work to do this evening, and Charlotte put her hand out toward Wini.

"Wini, Elsie is calling us—we can be one of the first ones to go inside of the tree. Are you ready?" Charlotte asked.

Duncan stood, leaned in, kissed Charlotte on the cheek and whispered, "I love you." He then hugged Tatiana tightly.

"Let's go!" Tatiana clapped her hands enthusiastically as Charlotte, Wini, and Lovey followed her to the entrance of the tree.

"'Bout time!" Elsie laughed, whisking them inside of the tree.

"Wow," Wini said with a sigh. Charlotte felt Wini's hand tighten around hers. They were now standing inside of the tree-shaped structure underneath thousands of lights every color imaginable. The twinkling of bright yellow, blue, red, green, purple, and every color of the rainbow gave the illusion of the Aurora Borealis. Brightly glowing yellow stars and white snowflakes dangled from the top of the structure on what seemed like invisible strings, creating pure Christmas magic.

"Tatiana, this is magnificent," Charlotte whispered, mesmerized by the beauty of the lights.

"It truly is. Harry is right—this is the best yet. That's the one thing about the Lobster Claw tree—you never know what it's going to be like from one year to the next. I'm not sure how Harry will top this one, though. What do you think, Wini?" Tatiana asked.

Other spectators milled about, but Wini stood in the center, turning around slowly, hypnotized by the sheer magnificence of the tree. The delightful seasonal melody of Tchaikovsky's Nutcracker was piped in, enhancing the beauty of the Christmas tree even more.

Wini's smile lit up her face as she patted Lovey's head, her eyes meeting Tatiana's and Charlotte's with joy.

"It's the most beautiful Christmas tree I have ever seen."

Charlotte bent down next to Lovey and looked at Wini, who was entranced by the magic.

"Me too," Charlotte whispered, smiling at Wini, secretly wishing this wonderful Christmas moment in Wini's young life would be something she would remember forever. Charlotte knew she'd never forget it.

"Oh!" exclaimed Tatiana, taking out her phone. "Let me get a picture of you three—the lighting is perfect."

Wini put her hand on top of Lovey's head, wrapping her other arm around Charlotte's waist. Charlotte lovingly looked at Wini, promising herself not to cry as an exuberant smile formed on the child's face.

"Beautiful!" Tatiana announced as she tapped her phone twice.

"Here," Elsie said, now wearing a Santa hat pulled over her bun and holding out her hand to Tatiana. "Give me your phone and hop in the picture."

Tatiana obliged and squatted behind Lovey as Elsie clicked away.

"Thank you, Elsie," Tatiana said. Elsie tipped her Santa hat and resumed her role of Lobster Claw Christmas tree photographer as others handed her their own phones for photos.

"I'm just going to quickly send these to Hamish, if you don't mind," Tatiana said, tapping her screen and smiling. "There," she nodded in affirmation. "He'll be here soon enough, but he said to send him photos from the tree lighting."

"Mission accomplished," Charlotte said, smiling. She heard Harry's loud voice through his megaphone.

"Listen up, everyone! I see our special visitors arriving now. Come on down to the north end of the dock and give them a huge Lobster Claw welcome!"

"Let's go," Tatiana said, and they each took one of Wini's hands and followed the crowd to the dock.

Harry frantically waved everyone toward the end as a faint light from the harbor began to appear. The children gasped in surprise as a boat picked up speed, the motor roaring. In the December night, the boat dazzled with flashing and twinkling lights, mirroring the brilliance of the tree. On top of the boat was the team of Santa's reindeer, with Rudolph in the lead, his red nose glowing as brightly as the Sea Star Lighthouse, blinking and winking at the cheers of the crowd. Parents lifted children upon shoulders, and everyone exuberantly called out the reindeer names.

"There's Rudolph!" one little boy shouted, waving his mittened hands furiously as the boat got closer to the dock. The reindeer were bobbing their heads up and down and back and forth as their legs kicked the boat closer to the dock.

Directly behind the reindeer was another boat—a familiar one —and Charlotte and Tatiana watched as Callum's Pride followed close behind the reindeer. Numerous lights and two Christmas trees adorned the beautiful Callum's Pride—one at the bow and another at the stern. Bright stars at the top of the trees twinkled as elves waved lanterns in the harbor breeze, the bells on the cuffs of their sleeves jingling in holiday merriment.

Duncan skillfully piloted the boat in the tranquil harbor. Santa Claus, full of cheer, waved with great enthusiasm. He had his own blow horn, and sang mirthfully, "Merry Christmas, Lobster Claw!"

Elsie, who was like a magical elf herself, changed into a long red velvet dress and cape, with white faux fur trim on the collar and cuffs, as the jolly old elf excited the children. Elsie's transformation into Mrs. Claus was absolutely remarkable. She held a basket of candy canes on her wrist and motioned for the children to form a line to talk to Santa next to an oversized green velvet chair.

Duncan docked the boat, then Santa and his elves stepped off and paraded down the dock, proclaiming Christmas cheer.

Tatiana, Charlotte, and Wini, along with Lovey, who was

behaving exceptionally well, watched Santa, in his big black boots, amble down the dock and seat himself on his throne.

"Charlotte," Tatiana whispered, as if she had seen a ghost. Wini's reaction preoccupied Charlotte, as the little girl remained fixated on Santa the entire time.

"Tatiana, are you alright?" Charlotte asked with concern in her voice. "What's wrong?"

Tatiana broke out into a huge smile. "Nothing is wrong, nothing at all. But don't you see? Santa?"

Charlotte looked toward the throne and realized what Tatiana had already known. That was no ordinary man dressed as Santa. It was the dear man they both loved.

"Well, Merry Christmas to you, Carter," Santa laughed as a little boy happily bounced from Santa's lap into the arms of his father. It was then that Charlotte heard the vague lilt of a Scottish accent, and she knew it was true—Hamish Falconer was sitting on Santa's throne, portraying the beloved Saint Nicholas of every child's dream.

"My Hamish," Tatiana murmured, and like Wini, she did not take her eyes from her beloved.

Charlotte shook her head in disbelief. "That man," she whispered back to Tatiana.

"Well, young lady," said Hamish, beckoning Wini, who was next in line.

Charlotte found it near impossible to stifle a laugh, knowing that the man behind the beard and inside the Santa suit looked nothing like Saint Nicholas.

"Are you ready, Wini?" Tatiana whispered, winking conspiratorially at Hamish, who returned the wink along with a cheerful smile for the woman he loved.

"Can Lovey come with me?" Wini asked, looking at Charlotte.

"Of course she can," Charlotte told her, handing over the lead. She took it and strolled up to Santa as if not believing this moment had finally arrived.

Lovey's tail wagged uncontrollably as she got closer to Hamish, and little whines of happiness and recognition escaped her as she practically climbed onto Hamish's lap herself.

"She must remember you from last year," Wini said, as Tatiana took the leash and brought Lovey over to the side of the throne to keep the secret safe.

"Good girl. Smart girl," Tatiana said, pulling one of her home-made dog treats from her pocket, which intrigued Lovey enough that her full attention was now on Tatiana's coat pocket.

"Well, I remember you, Wini," Hamish said, as the little girl positioned herself on his lap. "I hope you've been okay," he whispered. Hamish knew the full story, of course, and he wanted to be as kind and as gentle with Wini as possible.

"Thank you, Santa," Wini said. "I'm okay. I miss my mommy a lot, but she always told me that when she was going to live with the angels that she would always look over me and always be with me."

A spine-tingling chill ran through Charlotte upon hearing Wini's heartfelt words. As she watched her innocent face, she felt a surge of affection wash over her for this child, someone who lost so much, so young. *So beautiful,* she thought. *We all need to see things like Wini does. I know I do.* She then recalled her own paralyzing grief after Landon and Peppercorn died, and she had been nowhere near as adjusted as Wini was now. If it had not been for Hamish, she never would have recovered. Wini's mother prepared her well, making Charlotte realize Isobel had been an exceptional person and, above all, mother.

"That she is, Wini, that she is," Hamish said quietly. "Now, do you have any special requests for Christmas?"

Charlotte noticed Wini knitted her brows in deep thought. This characteristic was clear in both Duncan and Ivy when they were giving something thorough consideration, and she was right —Wini was a Kirk.

"Well, my Auntie Crys, I live with her now. She hurt herself today and couldn't come. Her ankle got twisted. I would wish for her ankle to get better soon. I do have another wish, Santa. Can I whisper it to you?"

"You most certainly can, Wini." Hamish bent his face down, and Wini cupped her hand over his ear and whispered her Christmas wish to Hamish. Charlotte thought she might be able to read Hamish's expression after Wini thanked him, but he gave his best belly laugh as Wini hopped off his knee.

"Don't forget your candy cane, Wini!" called Santa.

"Wini," Elsie said, "you forgot about your picture with Santa. Hop back up there and let's get Miss Charlotte and Miss Tatiana in there, too. And Lovey!"

Tatiana handed Elsie her phone, and Lovey lay between Santa's enormous boots, while Tatiana and Charlotte stood behind Santa, both with their hands on his shoulders.

"Say Merry Christmas!" Elsie chirped, and the little group happily obliged.

From the corner of her eye, Charlotte saw Tatiana bend down and give Hamish a quick kiss on the cheek. "Thank you, Santa," Charlotte whispered, leaving him with her own kiss. He winked, and Charlotte shook her head in astonishment, grateful that her cherished Hamish was back with them for Christmas.

"Did I miss a photo op with Santa?" Duncan asked, as he jogged toward the laughing group.

"That's okay, Duncan Donut," Wini said, the candy cane sticking out her mouth. "We can always come back tomorrow."

"That we will," he said, sweetly patting Wini on the head.

They approached the hot chocolate stand, and Duncan ordered for everyone. Benches lined the inside of the tree and they sat down and savored their hot drinks. Wini snuggled between Charlotte and Duncan, and they watched as Wini tilted her head upward to look at the illuminated stars and snowflakes. A smile formed on her face, and she took another sip of her drink.

"I wish Aunt Crys could see this," she said dreamily.

"Well, Chloe said the swelling should be down by tomorrow,

and if she's careful, she can come to see the tree. Does that sound good?" Charlotte asked, looking upward herself, mesmerized by the beautiful lights.

Wini nodded. "It does." She took another sip of her hot chocolate. "Does that boat belong to you, Duncan Donut?"

"It does. It was my father's boat, and he left it for me after he d —" Duncan stopped and rephrased what he was about to say. "After he went to be with the angels."

What a beautiful sentiment, Charlotte thought, thinking that Landon and Peppercorn were also "with the angels."

Wini drained her cup, leaving a little mustache upon her upper lip. "I've never been on a boat. It looked like Santa and the elves were having fun out there."

"You haven't?" Duncan asked. Charlotte could tell he was up to something by the sly smile forming on his face. "How would you like to go now? It's still early, and the harbor is calm. There's a full moon, and we could probably—"

"Really, truly? We can go now?" If Wini's hot chocolate cup wasn't empty, it would have soaked her pretty green coat. The excitement caused by Duncan's suggestion made her jump up rapidly.

"Really, truly." Duncan laughed, finishing the rest of his drink.

"Can Charlotte and Tatiana and Lovey come, too?"

"Thank you very much for asking me," Tatiana said, getting up. "But I would like to talk to Santa about some of my own Christmas wishes, and I need to get in that long line. You all go, and I will see you tomorrow," she said, blowing kisses to everyone. She turned around back to Wini and put some dog treats into Wini's hand. "Keep these in your pocket. Lovey loves them, and when she's a good girl, you can give her one."

"She's always good," Wini said. "Thank you."

"You all have fun and stay warm. I'll see you tomorrow." Tatiana bundled her tartan shawl tighter around her neck and shoulders and headed out to the line to wait for her visit with Santa.

"Who's ready for a boat ride?" Duncan asked, laughing and taking Wini's hand. He encircled Charlotte with his remaining arm, and she tightly grasped Lovey's leash as they made their way back to the dock for Wini's maiden voyage on Callum's Pride.

CHAPTER 26

PINK ANGEL

Duncan shut off the engine on Callum's Pride. They were a mile offshore, and the holiday lights of Lobster Claw were ablaze. The lobster trap Christmas tree sparkled brightly in the distance, and the light of Sea Star Lighthouse flashed back and forth. Duncan and Charlotte bundled up Wini and Lovey for their little adventure, as they had plenty of blankets on board to keep them warm in the cold weather.

"The moon is so pretty," Wini said. She was sitting next to Duncan, who remained behind the wheel.

"It's called the Cold Moon," Charlotte explained, pointing toward the beautiful and beaming moon. "If you look up during the December full moon, you can see how high in the sky it is. Since this is December 21st, it's also the shortest day of the year. The winter solstice moon takes the highest path into the sky, and it sits on top of the horizon longer than any other moon in the year —that's why it's the longest night. In a few nights, Santa's sleigh will take that same path. 'The moon on the breast of the new fallen snow gave the luster of midday to objects below,'" she concluded, quoting Clement C. Moore.

"That's from Dash Away," Wini said, smiling. "Auntie Crys

and I read Dash Away every night before I go to bed. We had to put a Santa Claus sticker on our calendar on December 1st to remind us to start." Wini giggled, her shoulders bouncing up and down in merriment. "I think it's more for Auntie Crys to remember. I would never forget something that important," she laughed.

Wini's reference to "'Twas the Night Before Christmas" made Charlotte smile. She thought it was simply adorable.

"Now, Dasher! Now, Dancer! Now, Prancer and Vixen," recited Charlotte. "On Comet, on Cupid, on Donder and Blitzen. To the top of the porch, to the top of the wall . . ."

"Now dash away, dash away, dash away all!" Wini happily finished as she and Charlotte fell into fits of laughter. "Do you think I'll be able to see Santa and his reindeer now that I know where to look?" Wini asked, gazing up at the beautiful moonlit Christmastime sky.

Duncan laughed. "Aren't you supposed to be asleep by then?"

Wini huddled closer to Duncan. Charlotte could see her eyelids were drooping, as if she were about to fall asleep.

"I am, but I always try to stay awake every year. Maybe I will this year," she said, taking one more look at the sky.

"Oh, look! A shooting star!" Charlotte cried, pointing upward. An arch of light bowed into the darkness as a trail of pink light followed. It was just a moment, but the shooting star's brevity was beautiful and breathtaking.

"It's the pink angel," Wini said, laying her head against Duncan's arm.

"What's a pink angel?" Duncan asked.

"I saw it once with my mommy. We were camping in the yard, and we were looking at the stars when a pink angel, like the one we just saw, flew across the sky. Mommy said it was the angel of kindness and love, and that if I saw it again, it meant she was looking over me.

Moved by Wini's simple perception, Charlotte whispered, "That's beautiful," acknowledging Wini's belief in the presence of her mother. Perhaps Isobel was watching over her daughter. Wini's eyes had closed, and she was now sleeping peacefully. Charlotte noticed her small hand was clutching onto Duncan's jacket as the boat bobbed gently in the serene harbor.

"The rocking of the ocean put her to sleep. It's calming. I remember my mother taking me into her lap when I was upset about something and sitting in her rocking chair slowly going back and forth, like now. When I found out that Landon and Peppercorn died, Hamish held me in his arms and gently rocked me like a baby. 'Shhh, shhh, Char,' he would whisper. 'All will be well again.' I never forgot that, and I know you won't forget this either, this moment, on the ocean, rocking your child to sleep." Charlotte moved beside Wini. Duncan's left hand caressed his daughter's strawberry blonde hair. He tightly wrapped his free arm around Charlotte and pulled her as close as possible. He buried his face in her wavy hair and kissed her lovingly.

"I don't know what I would do without you, Charlotte. Especially now. I truly don't."

When Charlotte looked into his hazel eyes, she noticed tears veiled them. She pressed her lips against his, savoring the taste of the salty night sea.

"I love you, Duncan," she whispered. "And no matter what happens with Wini, I will always be here for you. I promise."

Duncan pulled his arm from Charlotte. He removed the blanket from his lap, and set it under Wini's head, and laid her on the seat.

Although there was not much room on the boat, especially in the wheelhouse area, there was enough for Duncan to get down on bended knee. Charlotte felt his hands clasp around hers.

"Charlotte, I will never forget the first time we met in Elsie's. I think I fell in love with you right then. I never want to lose you, and I've had this for weeks, waiting for the right time. Ivy said I would know when it's right. And it's right now." Duncan reached into the pocket inside of his leather bomber jacket and held out a small black velvet box.

"Duncan," Charlotte whispered. This was something that she had not expected. She watched his thick fingers slowly lift the top of the box. Inside sat the most exquisite ring she had ever seen. It was a platinum gold band encrusted with brilliant star-like diamonds. Two emerald "leaves" surrounded a pink sapphire that was in the shape of a rose.

"Charlotte Templeton," Duncan quietly said, "will you marry me?"

She saw nothing but love in his hazel eyes, and she didn't know which was more brilliant at this moment—the ring or his eyes. Those kind eyes that shone back at her on that stormy May night in Elsie's Everything. He was her knight in shining armor then, and she wanted him to be that for the rest of their lives.

"Yes, Duncan Kirk. I will marry you."

She watched as he then lifted the ring from the soft velvet box, as the beating of her heart echoed in her ears. He took her trembling hand in his and lovingly placed the ring on Charlotte's finger.

Charlotte extended her hand underneath the moonlight, watching the ring sparkle and glow as the moonbeams shimmered upon it.

Duncan stood, his arms extended. Charlotte got up and melted into his body, feeling his strong arms enveloped her in a passionate embrace. She gazed up into his adoring eyes and then felt his lips gently press upon hers, igniting a surge of electricity within Charlotte. She fervently returned his kiss, never wanting this moment to end.

Under the alluring, starry December sky, she was in the embrace of the man she loved to the very depth of her soul. She cuddled deeper into him as another shooting star streaked across the heavens, its ethereal pink glow illuminating the winter night.

CHAPTER 27

TOO FAST

"I still cannot believe this!" Tatiana said. She and Hamish relaxed in worn wing chairs inside of The Blue Hydrangea, complete with a fresh pot of tea and chocolate biscuits.

She lovingly looked at Hamish. "If I had known you were coming, I would have made your cinnamon scones. But these little cookies will have to do." Her smile hadn't faded since she discovered the Lobster Claw Santa was actually Hamish Falconer. When Tatiana looked at Hamish, it felt as if she was seeing him for the first time, just like at McGilvery's pub years ago.

Hamish took a generous sip of his tea. "Ah, Tati, you still make the best tea. The Chai doesn't taste the same without you in Scotland." He took a nibble of the chocolate cookie. "Delicious as well."

A rush of love coursed through her body as she gazed at the man who she undeniably loved. Her gaze then shifted towards Annabelle's portrait. Annabelle and Hamish bore a striking resemblance, much like Duncan and Wini, from their chin dimples to their round blueberry eyes.

"She's always with us, love," Hamish whispered, following Tatiana's glance toward Annabelle's portrait.

Tatiana nodded. "She is. Now, how on Earth did you pull off this Christmas surprise?" She savored a cookie, waiting to hear Hamish's explanation.

Hamish put his mug down and looked directly at her. "It all began after you left. Seven weeks seemed like an eternity. Nothing was the same without you—the walks, the tea, the talks. I thought golfing and playing with Lachlan would help ease my loneliness, but it only made me miss you more. You weren't waiting for me at the clubhouse when I returned from golfing, with your big, beautiful smile. You weren't there when I played with Lachlan in the yard with his own golf clubs. Your absence made me feel lost, and I realized I didn't want to be away from you. So, I shared my plan with Colin and …"

Hamish stopped and Tatiana saw his jaw tense.

"What did Colin say, Hamish?" Tatiana recognized the distressed look on Hamish's face. The ruddiness became pale, and he cast his eyes downward, telltale signs that something had transpired between father and son.

"He thinks I'm moving too fast."

Tatiana felt her heart drop and her hands trembled. "Hamish, I never want to be the reason for any distance between you and Colin. That would devastate me."

Hamish brought his chair closer, and she felt tears fill her eyes. His comforting hand, with its rough texture, gently brushed against her cheek, and she knew he was trying to console her.

"I told him, in no uncertain terms, that I was not moving too fast, and that I will not lose another minute. He was disappointed that I wanted to come back to Maine for Christmas, but he and Haleigh were going to spend it in London anyway, with her sister who has a son Lachlan's age. My absence would go completely unnoticed. He said that wasn't the point. Being back in Scotland with them made him happy, and he wanted us all together for Christmas. I think he was trying to make me feel guilty, but I didn't let it get to me. Haleigh agreed with me, and she'll make sure he comes around. He does adore you, Tati, but the reality of you and me together is hitting him now. It's hard for him to understand, and I know he wants me to be there for Lachlan, too. But whatever time I have left on this Earth, I want to spend it with you. That's what I know." Tatiana could feel Hamish's breath as he leaned over, pressing his gentle kiss upon her lips.

"Oh, Hamish, I want that, too. But I don't want any discord between you and your son. Promise me you'll get this resolved. I couldn't bear anything happening between you and Colin."

"I promise. I hesitated to tell you, but I believe in being open with you," he said.

Tatiana felt the tough skin of his thumb on her cheek as he brushed away a tear that had fallen. She took Hamish's hand to her lips. "I know," she whispered, thinking about that time in the past when she hid a secret from him, only to realize she couldn't keep it to herself.

"I promise. All will be well."

Hamish's smile always made her worries vanish. She knew he was right, and she found herself excited for her first Christmas with him.

"Now, going back to your original question of how I kept this a secret," Hamish said, laughing. "Duncan is good at keeping secrets, unlike Charlotte. If she caught wind of my intention to visit Lobster Claw, she would have informed you. He needed someone to play Santa for the boat parade, and I offered to be his guy. I arrived this morning and have been holding up at Duncan's all day."

In her own seven decades on Earth, Tatiana had never been more surprised or felt more loved. She made a silent promise to never leave Hamish again, and after talking with Hamish, she was confident that Colin would eventually understand his father's choice. It might take some time, but she believed Colin would come around.

Tatiana decided to remove all worries from her mind—there

was nothing she could do about them just a few days before Christmas, and she wanted to focus solely on the one thing that mattered most to her, which was spending Christmas with Hamish. This Christmas would mark the beginning of many Christmases they would celebrate together.

CHAPTER 28

ONCE WE'RE MARRIED

The jam-packed weekend flew by quickly. With Wini and Crystal's visit, opening the store, and preparing for Christmas, Charlotte barely had a moment to process her engagement to Duncan.

Charlotte and Duncan planned to keep the ring and engagement a secret until Christmas Day. They would be spending Christmas at Tatiana's, where they planned to announce their news. Ivy and Andy would join them for dessert after having Christmas dinner with Andy's family. Ivy was the only one who knew about the ring, and Charlotte knew from Duncan's almost childlike excitement that he could not wait to see his sister's reaction when she saw it on Charlotte's finger.

Tourists milled about the Beach Block, but most were headed to the holiday festivities at Snow Cap Mountain. Figuring she wasn't losing too much revenue, Charlotte decided to close the shop early. Now, in the twilight of Christmas Eve, Charlotte settled herself on the couch to enjoy a quiet glass of wine. Lovey hopped up next to her and settled her sweet head into Charlotte's lap. The bungalow was cozy and warm, and the candles and Christmas tree lights added a comfy and festive touch. Duncan was late due to a delivery in Camden but would be home by eight. The tranquil seas enabled him to still ferry, and until they turned stormy, he planned to keep sailing.

Charlotte sipped her wine, looking forward to their walk on the beach. They planned to go by the Beach Block and to the lobster trap Christmas tree, and then stop in at Tatiana's for a Christmas Eve toast of Tatiana's homemade eggnog.

Crystal and Wini had left for home on the 23rd. Crystal's ankle swelling had decreased considerably, giving her the ability to walk, along with a cane Chloe insisted she take "just in case." Duncan received a text from her thanking him for a wonderful time, and assuring him she would be in touch after the New Year. Even though Wini had been there for just a weekend, Charlotte sharply felt her absence. Gone was the Christmas enthusiasm that only a child can bring, and the innocence and energy of an eight-year-old child at this time of the year was infectious. A pang of melancholy rolled in her stomach, and she was surprised that she missed Wini as much as she did. A shiver of loneliness coursed through her, and a bite of sadness pierced her heart. She had the special experience of spending time with a child at Christmas, and she genuinely missed Wini.

Charlotte's gaze shifted to her finger, to the stunningly beautiful ring. Her hand swayed, and she was captivated by the sparkling diamonds, shimmering emerald leaves, and breathtaking pink sapphire rose. The engagement ring was so beautiful, she never wanted to remove it, but remembered she needed to before going to Tatiana's. Looking at the ring, she knew how loved she was. Duncan brought so much love and joy into her life. Her grip of sadness was released, and she knew Wini would be back before she knew it.

Charlotte got up and walked upstairs to her bedroom loft. From the top drawer of her dresser, she retrieved the brown velvet box that was found in Landon's glove compartment the day he died. She opened the box and looked at her other engagement ring —a beautiful oval emerald surrounded by twelve diamonds. In the

Christmas Eve twilight, the dazzling ring brought back memories of a special man and his beloved dog, banishing all traces of sorrow. In an amazing turn of events, another man and dog entered her life, proving to Charlotte that life and love can start anew. Bringing the emerald ring to her lips, Charlotte kissed it, returned it to the box, and slipped it back into the drawer. Perhaps in the future, she may find someone to give the ring to, but for now, it remained in its special place in the drawer and in her heart.

Lovey bellowed from downstairs as the familiar sound of Duncan's truck pulled in front of the bungalow.

With a quick glance in the mirror, Charlotte fluffed her hair and rushed down the stairs, eagerly opening the door. Lovey dashed out, exuberantly jumping around upon seeing one of her favorite people arrive.

"Merry Christmas Eve, fiancée," Duncan said, walking into the toasty bungalow with Lovey at his heels. She couldn't wait for that bomber jacket embrace and rushed into his arms. His lips found hers in a passionate kiss.

"Merry Christmas Eve, fiancé," Charlotte chimed back. "I like how it sounds," she said, secure in his embrace. "You even smell like Christmas." The rich aroma of freshly cut pine enveloped the bungalow, courtesy of his aftershave. Duncan laughed that hearty and happy laugh that made Charlotte weak in her knees, and she felt his hug tighten.

"And you're the best Christmas present I ever got," he said. "If I never receive another Christmas gift, it won't matter, because once we're married, it will feel like Christmas every day."

"Once we're married," Charlotte repeated. "I like the sound of that, too."

CHAPTER 29

A smile formed on Crystal's lips as she watched Wini ensconced inside a mountain of Christmas wrapping paper. Everything from Wini's Christmas list and more was scattered in the living room, as Crystal wanted to make sure, especially this Christmas, it would be a wonderful one.

Crystal, her ankle still tender but significantly improved, sat on the couch, sipping a cup of coffee. Wini's excitement was palpable as she tore into beautifully wrapped packages, her arms flailing in delight with each gift. Beading and crochet kits, puzzles, and her favorite colored pens, and coloring books all elicited happy "oooohs" and "ahhhs," along with a multitude of thankful hugs and kisses. But there was still one more gift she needed to give to Wini. "Sweetie, come here. I have a special present for you."

"I have something for you too," Wini said, going back to the Christmas tree and picking up a wrapped rectangular box. "You open yours first," she said with a smile, handing Crystal the box.

The package was wrapped in festive silver foil, decorated with Christmas stickers, and expertly tied with a green ribbon.

"This is beautiful, Wini," Crystal said softly.

Wini smiled shyly. "I didn't wrap it. Charlotte did. But I picked this out especially for you."

Charlotte did. Crystal felt a brief sting as an arrow of envy pierced her ears. Because she was bed bound, Crystal was hardly involved in their weekend in Lobster Claw. Duncan, Charlotte, Lovey, and now Tatiana were all her young grandniece could talk about. As much as Crystal wanted to be happy for Wini, a tiny wisp of fear of losing her remained in the back of her mind.

Crystal slowly unwrapped the gift. She opened the box and inside was a garland of seashells laying upon white tissue paper. Crystal gently lifted it from the box, and a symphony of tinkling bells jingled in her hands. Each shell threaded upon the garland was unique and had its own distinct color. The beauty of the gift touched Crystal.

"Wini, this is absolutely beautiful. Where did you get it?"

"Charlotte told me I could pick something for you from her store. It's such a pretty store, Aunt Crys. It was all decorated for Christmas, too. She had these on her little Christmas tree, and I thought they were so pretty, especially the little bells. Charlotte told me that when she took over the store, she found a box of them, and that she taught herself how to make more. I think she maybe made this one, but I'm not sure. I hope you like it." Wini's grin was as wide as the seashell garland Crystal was holding in her hand.

"I love it," she said, ensconcing Wini in an enormous hug. "Let's find a special spot to hang this. What do you think?"

Wini nodded in agreement, her head swiveling around the living room like an owl perched on a tree branch, trying to decide on the perfect place.

"But before we do, I have one more gift for you." Crystal leaned forward and pulled a box from behind the pillow she was leaning on. There was a card attached to the top of the box.

"Is this from Mommy?" Wini asked incredulously, instantly recognizing Isobel's handwriting on the envelope of the card.

"It is," Crystal said.

Wini gently took the card and opened the envelope. She slowly pulled out the card. The front of the card had a woman and a girl, sitting under a brightly decorated Christmas tree. The card had "To my daughter at Christmas" written in green script. Wini opened the card and read what was written inside.

My dearest Wini,

Merry Christmas! The best Christmas present I could ever give you is all of my love forever and forever. You were always my best birthday present and best Christmas present, and there is no one in the world that I love more than you. This Christmas present is very special, and I hope you will always have it with you as a reminder of me and of you. Remember, my beautiful Wini, I will always be with you. I love you forever and forever. Merry Christmas.

Love, Mommy.

"I miss Mommy. But I know she's here with us today," Wini said.

Crystal saw a small smile form on her niece's face. She had prepared herself for tears, but none came, leaving her more in awe of Wini than she ever had been. Instead of tears of sadness, Wini's smile was one of pure joy and happiness. Despite not being able to spend this special holiday with her daughter, Isobel ensured that Wini's first Christmas without her would be special.

Wini gingerly removed the wrapping paper and within her hand was a cream-colored octagonal jewelry case with pink flowers and tiny blue birds painted on it.

"Mommy's jewelry box!" Wini gasped in utter delight.

Wini had long admired Isobel's jewelry box, one that Isobel received herself from Santa when she was Wini's age. She slowly pulled up the gold clasp on the front of the box and lifted the lid. As she did, a twinkle of a melody played, and a ballerina twirled. Opening the box always fascinated Wini with the dancing ballerina and the pretty music that emanated from it. Crystal was pleased that Wini still experienced the same enchantment with the box as she always had when her mother was still alive.

"Mommy said that one day I could have it," Wini quietly said, cradling the precious jewelry box in her small hands.

"I think there might be something else in there." Crystal watched Wini's mouth form into a perfect O. Sitting inside the soft pink plush of the box was Isobel's favorite piece of jewelry.

"Mommy's locket." Wini picked up the heart-shaped locket, which was dancing from a gold chain that glistened in the Christmas morning light. There was a cloisonné painting of a pink flower, two green leaves on a brown stem, with a gold background. Her tiny fingers carefully opened the locket to a photograph nestled inside.

"It's me and Mommy. Can you put it on me, please?"

Crystal took the locket and pulled Wini's strawberry blonde hair from her neck. She secured the clasp, and Wini's hair fell gently back onto her shoulders, framing her locket perfectly.

"You look stunning," Crystal said, barely able to hold back tears.

Despite the difficult circumstances, Wini found joy and love in the presence of her mother during Christmas. Isobel had instilled in Wini the confidence that she would always be loved, even without Isobel's physical presence. And what a job she had done.

"See," Wini said, cradling the locket in her hands, "now Mommy will really and truly always be with me."

"Yes, sweetie, she really will be," Crystal whispered as a wave of regret and anger washed over her, causing her body to tremble. "We better get ready for church and the Christmas party afterward."

"Woo hoo," Wini cried, as the excitement of the Christmas party now occupied Wini's thoughts. "Merry Christmas, Auntie Crys. I love you."

Wini's arms tightly embraced her, and Crystal swore she could feel the power of this child's love flow into her. Then, quick as the proverbial bunny, Wini jumped off the couch and headed to her bedroom to get ready.

You silly woman, she thought. Crystal's fear of Wini and Duncan's relationship overpowered her. It was foolish of her to actually believe that Wini would just decide to leave her home and her grandaunt. She and her niece shared an inseparable bond, deeply connected in heart and soul. She, Wini, and Isobel had been living in their own little untouchable bubble that burst when Isobel died. Then she and Wini created another one with just the two of them. However, Isobel wanted Duncan to know about Wini, and she left it for him, not Crystal, to decide if he wanted Wini in his life. Confident that he wouldn't be interested in a child, Crystal had underestimated his integrity, and this had frightened her. When she was laid up in Chloe's B&B with her painful ankle, her mind had wandered into its darkest recesses. Could this new dynamic work? Would it only be during vacations that they would see each other? Would that only confuse Wini? Her mind had been awash in doubts and fear, and she could not think straight. Crystal felt ashamed as she realized that Wini, at just eight years old, had been stronger than she. Acting more childlike than Wini, she was hesitant to let anyone enter their private little world. Now that she had, she discovered that their world would not end; it would only become more enriched with Duncan in it.

Just then, the clear and angelic sound of Wini singing "Jingle Bells" permeated the Christmas morning. Crystal shared in the happiness radiating from her voice. She was no longer the dejected and woebegone aunt who was about to be left out in the winter cold. Crystal never truly was that. Their family was expanding, and there undoubtedly was no better Christmas gift than that.

She then remembered the gift that Duncan sent via overnight mail for Wini, as he wanted it to be a surprise on Christmas morning. She slowly walked to her bedroom and using Chloe's cane, she swished it from under her bed, sweeping the beautifully wrapped box out from beneath it. "Ouch," she said, bending down and picking up the gift. She hobbled back into the living room and placed the gift under the tree, concealing it among the wrapping paper still left on the floor from the other gifts. Once they arrived home after the Christmas party, she would pretend to clean and stumble across a surprise gift for Wini under the tree. *She'll be thrilled*, Crystal thought. A twinge of pain emanated from her ankle, and she was about to grab her cane. She laughed and said, "Canes are for old women," and went back to her room without it. Crystal's dependence on Wini, much like her reliance on the cane, had reached its end, and she was up for the challenge of new beginnings on this Christmas Day.

CHAPTER 30

HALF-WAY TO ONE YEAR

"Merry Christmas, everyone." Hamish Falconer toasted around Tatiana's dining room table. Charlotte beamed with love as she clinked glasses of champagne with Hamish, Tatiana, and Duncan. A festive plaid runner, red bayberry candles, and pine boughs adorned with pinecones made for a stylish setting. Gold forks and knives sat on each side of the plates on coordinated placemats, and crystal water glasses and red wine goblets finished the merry table setting.

"Merry Christmas," they all chimed in response.

To honor her Polish roots, Tatiana had prepared a delectable mushroom soup, along with a ham spiked with cloves and pineapples. Charlotte prepared the sides of stuffing and mashed potatoes, and desserts of a mile-high apple pie and coconut cream cake were courtesy of Take the Cake Bakery.

The foursome enjoyed their first Christmas dinner together. Tatiana and Hamish handled the dishwasher duty while Duncan and Charlotte took care of setting the table for dessert. Tatiana had a teapot that matched her Christmas china, along with four cups and saucers that Charlotte put on the table with care.

"Tatiana, we're just going to take Lovey out for a quick walk. Table's all set for dessert," Charlotte announced as she put her coat on.

"Perfect. Take your time. I'm going to start the tea and coffee, so when you three get back, dessert will be served." Tatiana pet Lovey and bent down and whispered, "And don't you worry, sweetie, I have a special treat for you, too." Lovey wagged her tail wildly and kissed Tatiana enthusiastically on her cheeks.

It was close to five o'clock when Duncan and Charlotte left with Lovey. Charlotte stood outside of The Blue Hydrangea and looked up and down the Beach Block. It was as still as the middle of the night—not one person in sight on this beautiful and silent night. She glanced skyward and saw the first formation of stars beginning to twinkle with a hint of a sliver of the silver moon.

"Penny for your thoughts," Duncan said, wrapping his arm around Charlotte.

She pulled his arm tighter around her shoulder as they started to walk toward the shore.

"I sometimes feel I still have to pinch myself to make sure this is real," Charlotte said, looking into Duncan's smiling hazel eyes. "My life was in shambles, losing my job, my home. Hamish leaving, or so I thought." She chuckled. "I feel like this little town has been more of a home to me than even my cottage on the golf course, which I loved with all my heart. The people, Ivy, Tatiana, Lovey—you. You were the biggest surprise of all," she said, tears prickling her eyes. But they were not tears of sadness; they were of pure joy and happiness.

"I know," Duncan said. Charlotte let Lovey off her leash, as they were now on the beach. "I was such a mess when I came back here, and then I almost left. I would have, if it weren't for this beautiful woman I saw in Elsie's who was on some kind of crazy mission." He smiled down at her. "And when I saw your face, well, there was no way I was leaving. I knew an opportunity to help a beautiful damsel in distress doesn't come around like that often."

Charlotte smiled, listening to Duncan recall the night they met over six months ago. Halfway to one year. Charlotte watched her other unexpected gift, Lovey, who had trotted a little further ahead.

The night was cold and bright, with a million stars shining down on them, illuminated with the beam from Sea Star Lighthouse. A stiff wind blew, and the freezing air chilled Charlotte to the bone.

"Let's head back, Duncan," Charlotte said. "It's colder than I thought." His arms tightened around her as a sense of love and security rushed through her. "C'mon, Lovey, time for dessert."

Lovey wasted no time in joining them for their walk back to The Blue Hydrangea.

"Oh, don't forget the ring," Duncan said as they stood in front of Tatiana's.

Charlotte had been true in keeping it a secret and hadn't worn it in public—as much as she wanted to.

"Right here," Charlotte smiled as she reached into the inside pocket of her coat. She handed the box to Duncan.

"Can you put it on me, please?" She smiled, her heart quickening as he took the box from her.

"I'll do more than that," he said, kneeling before her, laughing, and he opened the box.

"Charlotte Templeton, will you marry me?"

"Can I have some time to think it over?" she teased as he took her hand and placed the ring back on her finger again.

"Absolutely not," he whispered, and his smile melted Charlotte's heart. He rose from his bended knee and was now standing before her.

She closed her eyes in anticipation of his kiss, a kiss that always filled her with love. Quivers ran throughout her, and the love she felt bewitched her body and soul. Charlotte knew he was the perfect man for her.

"Ready?" he whispered, opening the door and escorting Lovey and Charlotte back inside.

"As I'll ever be." She smiled as she looked adoringly at the man who soon would be her husband.

CHAPTER 31

CHRISTMAS WITHOUT YOU

"That was a Christmas to beat all Christmases, Tati," Hamish said, putting his hands on Tatiana's cheeks and kissing her softly. The aroma of freshly brewed coffee filled Tatiana's apartment as they waited for Charlotte, Duncan, and Lovey to return from their walk.

"I still can't believe you're here," Tatiana murmured. She could feel her heart accelerate a bit as she prepared herself to ask her next question. "Are you missing your family?" She stepped away from him to the other side of the kitchen counter and occupied herself by cutting the pie and the cake, not wanting to make direct eye contact with him. She knew if she did, she could see if there was truth or lies in his eyes. She then felt his nearness, hearing his footsteps behind her. His sturdy hand removed the cake knife from hers. He placed his hands on her shoulders and turned her around. His leathery hand then caressed her face, sending a thrill through her body. She looked into his eyes and saw the truth gleaming in them.

"I would not have missed Christmas with you. Even if Colin and Haleigh were at home, I still would have come to Maine. You mean everything to me, and I am not missing any more Christmases, New Years, Easters, Fourth of Julys—I will not miss any holidays with you ever again." He softly kissed her forehead. "And that's another thing I wanted to talk to you about."

Hearing the door open downstairs brought Hamish's words to a stop. "We'll talk later," he whispered, interrupted by the return of their friends.

Tatiana squeezed his hand in affirmation and smiled. "Yes, my Hamish," she whispered back. "Perfect timing, you two," Tatiana announced as Charlotte, Duncan, and Lovey arrived back in the apartment.

They sat down at the table, and Tatiana passed around the dessert plates she'd filled with cake and pie. Charlotte took her plate from Tatiana, who quickly did a double take.

"Put that plate down, young lady," she commanded, "and hold out your hand. Why am I only now noticing this?" she asked incredulously, because a stunning ring like the one on Charlotte's finger was impossible to ignore.

She smiled as she saw Charlotte's face reddened with sheer happiness.

Duncan took one of the dessert knives and gently tapped it on his crystal water glass.

"If I may have your attention, please," he began. "I have asked Charlotte to marry me, and she said yes!"

Hamish quickly rose from his chair and hugged his dear friend. "I am so happy for you, Char," he said, kissing her on her tear-stained cheek. "Char." Hamish wiped away tears from Charlotte's cheeks. "Why the tears, dear?" he asked tenderly.

"Hamish, you've been with me through everything, everything good and everything horrible. It's because of you I found my way to Lobster Claw, and I found my way to the people I now love more than anything in the world. You're my guardian angel, my fairy godfather. You're everything to me and I love you so much. None of this," she said, looking around the room, "would have happened without you. There was a time when I never thought I'd be happy again, but I am, thanks to you. Merry Christmas, Hamish."

"Oh, Char, you trying to make me cry, too?" Hamish took Charlotte's hands in his own. "If it weren't for you, I would have never found Tati again, so I'd say we're even."

"There is a reason you came to Lobster Claw, Charlotte," Tatiana said softly. "And we are all the reason."

"I can't speak for everyone else, but I'm definitely ready for dessert." Duncan chuckled, and the mood instantly lightened.

"Aye, aye!" shouted Hamish, as the four sat down to enjoy their Christmas dessert.

A knock on the front door halted Tatiana from taking her place at the table. "I'll get that, and she went downstairs."

"Merry Christmas," Ivy said cheerily from the other side of the door. "Sorry if we are a bit late, but—"

"When my family gets together, it's tough to escape," Andy interrupted. "But we did and here we are."

"Wonderful," Tatiana said, ushering them upstairs. "Get inside and warm up. It's cold out there. Tatiana took their coats. "Ivy, take a seat and I'll get anything that you want."

"Thanks so much," Ivy said as she sat down on the couch. Andy joined his wife as Tatiana passed the plates full of delicious pie and cake. After taking a bite, Ivy set her plate aside. She then reached for Andy's hand and placed it on her belly. "This baby is going to have a sweet tooth," Ivy declared. "One bite of cake and this little guy or girl is kicking up a storm."

Seeing a pregnant Ivy with her husband's hand on her belly warmed Tatiana's heart. Knowing that this child would be welcomed into a home with parents who would love him or her deeply as she had loved her own daughter. She never experienced Christmases with a child of her own, but with Wini, Lachlan, and now Ivy's baby, perhaps she would.

"Merry Christmas, my dear." Hamish whispered into her ear. "It's our first of many. I promise you that."

Tatiana looked into the eyes of the man she had loved for most of her life. She laid her head upon his shoulder and felt the softness of his flannel shirt on her cheek. She swore she smelled the leather of his favorite chair back at his home in Scotland, along with the sweet fragrance of cinnamon from the scones he loved. She would cherish this moment for the rest of her life—the moment that marked her first Christmas with Hamish Falconer. A Christmas she had waited a lifetime for.

CHAPTER 32

ALMOST CHARLOTTE KIRK

The New Year was heralded into Lobster Claw with one of Harry's iconic bonfires and a breathtaking fireworks spectacle.

New Year's Day began with the intrepid Duncan, Hamish, and Lovey taking part in the fiftieth annual Lobster Claw Beach Block Beach Bath, where brave souls from Lobster Claw and the surrounding communities partook in diving into the winter waves of the Atlantic Ocean. Hamish, who stayed in the longest, received the honors for Best of the Beach Block Beach Bath this year.

"It's all that Scotch whisky in your blood, Hamish," Harry joked, being knocked off the pedestal from last year. Harry handed Hamish a large beach blanket adorned with a Lobster Claw motif, and the two champions warmly shook hands.

"Haven't touched a drop of that in years," Hamish said with a laugh, pulling the blanket tighter around his shoulders. "But I shall cherish this blanket, especially now." Lovey had also won in the canine category, which wasn't a surprise to anyone, as she truly loved the ocean, no matter what the temperature.

During January, Charlotte was busy with her regular work tasks, ordering inventory for the upcoming season, getting rid of items that didn't sell well, and coming up with new ideas and testing products for the influx of tourists who would visit Snow Cap for the February school vacation. Snow Cap offered a winter day-camp for children, giving parents the opportunity to hit the slopes or visit Lobster Claw for some shopping while their kids were engaged in activities.

Charlotte placed an order for additional key chains, coasters, and T-shirts. She also set up a kids' corner in the store, where children could relax, read, or color while their parents explored The Shop at Beach Rose Path.

"Good time to try it out," she said to Duncan one day as he was helping her move a large table she ordered from Camden that had arrived. It was a picnic table, with a bench on each side, which would comfortably fit six children. She stocked up on coloring books and various coloring supplies, like colored pencils, markers, and crayons.

"I think it's a great idea," Duncan said, carefully setting the heavy benches on each side of the table. "I also have another great idea." He sat on the bench and motioned for Charlotte to sit beside him.

"I love your great ideas," Charlotte said with a smile, sitting down next to him. "What are you thinking?"

"How about inviting Wini to come to spend her winter break here? I think she'd like it, and we might take her up to Snow Cap for a day. Maybe she could help around here? What do you think?"

"That is a great idea. I can definitely use an extra pair of hands. Maybe I can put her to work helping with the kids and coloring with them? She had fun in the store at Christmas. I think she'd really like it."

"I was hoping you would say that." Duncan leaned over and kissed her on the forehead.

"Why wouldn't I? You know I adore her. Were you thinking of asking Crystal as well?"

"I was thinking I'd leave that up to Crystal. She's more than welcome, of course, but I also want her to feel that Wini is in excellent hands with us."

Charlotte nodded in agreement. "I love it. I'll leave the planning to you, but let me know if you need me to do anything. Wini is welcome to stay here, too. She can have the loft, and I can sleep on my comfy couch. I think she'd love the view of Sea Star Lighthouse."

"You're amazing, Charlotte Templeton, almost Charlotte Kirk," Duncan said, taking her hands and tenderly kissing them. "I'll give Crystal a call," he said, getting up from the bench to step outside and take advantage of better cell reception.

She watched Duncan talk on the phone outside as flurries softly drifted down onto the brown ground. A cloud of snow had floated through the pale blue sky as the haziness of winter sunshine filtered through the clouds. Flurries as downy as angel wings drifted down from the heavens, alighting onto Duncan's hair, as well as the shoulders of his cherished and weathered bomber jacket. She heard the bright chirps of the cardinals and the chickadees flutter through the now bare branches of the oak trees. They playfully flittered and flickered in the wan winter sunshine, occasionally pecking a branch for any tidbit of food. Her attention returned to Duncan, who smiled and nodded his head happily. He gave the thumbs up and blew her a kiss.

February vacation was still weeks away, but her thoughts were in motion. Determined to make Wini's visit as enjoyable as Christmas, she picked up her trusted notebook and started devising a plan on how to keep her entertained. And just like that, one of her least favorite months started to look a little bit warmer and brighter with the prospect of a little houseguest.

CHAPTER 33

COME BACK QUICKLY

"What do you think?" Charlotte asked, revealing her newly decorated loft. She dedicated the last few weeks revamping it, making sure it was perfect for Wini.

"Charlotte, this looks absolutely gorgeous," Tatiana said, standing in the loft as they prepared for Wini's arrival the next day.

"I thought she might enjoy this," Charlotte said, smoothing out the pretty new pink flowered quilt she placed on her bed. In addition, she bought sheets and pillowcases that matched, creating an ambiance of a young girl's space in the loft.

"Oh, and I added these, too." Charlotte moved to the small table near the window and flicked a switch. The room filled with a soft glow from small pastel lights that adorned the window frames and bed headboard.

"It's simply magical. Can I move in here after Wini goes home?" Tatiana laughed, admiring the enchantment that Charlotte brought to the loft for her young visitor.

"No kidding. I think I'm going to keep them up even after she leaves," she said, turning off the switch. "I hope she likes it."

Tatiana shook her head. "She will love it. Don't you worry

about that. Also, I was thinking it would be great to have Wini visit the gallery, if that's okay with you."

"Oh, I think she'd *love* that, too," Charlotte said, satisfied with loft's new look. "Duncan says Wini is very excited, especially staying in the loft with Lovey."

"Will Crystal be joining her?" Tatiana asked.

"Crystal is coming up on the train and spending the night at the B&B, and then she's heading back to Newport. The airline she used to work for asked her to do some kind of training because one of their senior flight attendants had a family issue and won't be able to do it. Talk about perfect timing."

"Well, Crystal can rest assured Wini will be well taken care of." Tatiana embraced Charlotte and checked her watch. "Oh, gotta get back to the gallery. Hamish is supposed to FaceTime me in fifteen minutes. Have to make sure my own face is ready." She laughed.

Hamish had returned to Scotland on the second of January and intended to return to Lobster Claw in March. He and Tatiana had a long discussion of what they wanted for their future. It was his goal to make good use of the winter months to ensure all of his affairs in Scotland were in order.

"Let him know I said hello and to come back quickly. I'll text him myself later," Charlotte said while she and Tatiana made their way downstairs.

Lovey got up from her bed and kissed Tatiana's hand, and she gave the precious pup one of her favorite treats.

Tatiana kissed Charlotte on the cheek. "I will. Text if you need anything."

"Thanks," Charlotte said, watching Tatiana walk down the wooden dock back to the Beach Block.

"Okay," Charlotte said to Lovey, who was wagging her tail in excitement. "We still have a little work to do, and then it will be time for our walk." Lovey happily settled back in her corner and chewed on her rawhide as Charlotte finished up her chores.

CHAPTER 34

REUNION

Over the past few weeks since returning to Newport, Crystal became kinder to herself, allowing herself to realize Duncan presented a positive change in their lives. Listening to Wini's phone conversations with Duncan, discussing violin lessons and what she had for lunch, Crystal recognized Duncan's uplifting effect on Wini. Their chats were clearly anticipated, as Wini always ended the call with, "Can't wait to talk next week."

Her own conversations with Duncan calmed her worries and gave her confidence in his ability to be a good dad. But only time could tell if Duncan had the qualities of an excellent father, and Crystal believed that Wini's February vacation would be a good barometer of his parenting skills.

When Isobel returned to Newport to raise Wini, Crystal decided to semi-retire as a senior flight attendant for Coastal Atlantic Airways, a subsidiary of a larger international carrier, Atlantic Air Service. Recently, one of their veteran flight attendant instructors had a family emergency, and the airline asked her to substitute. The training facility was in Albany, New York, and Crystal only needed to be there for two days. Although her apprehension about losing Wini had decreased dramatically since Christmas, she couldn't deny that a small flicker of fear occasionally crept into her mind, making her feel slightly uneasy. But Wini's loving hugs would then instantly erase her fears.

Still, these thoughts flitted around like pesky mosquitoes on a scorching summer day as they rode the train to Brunswick. Wini passed the time on the train ride by reading a book, while Duncan's Christmas gift, a stuffed yellow Labrador, affectionately called LJ, short for Lovey Jr., cuddled up next to her. While Crystal looked on, Wini softly read to LJ, simultaneously pointing to the illustrations that showcased the thrilling adventures of a black-and-white cat and a yellow dog. Wini cherished the stuffed animal, and LJ was her constant companion. She'd used some of her Christmas money to shop for a larger school backpack that could comfortably fit LJ inside. Wini left the backpack unzipped so that LJ could breathe when they went to school together.

Wini rested her head on the back of the train seat. As her eyes closed, she instinctively nestled LJ closer to her side. There was still an hour and a half left before arriving in Brunswick, and a nap wasn't a bad idea. Taking a cue from Wini, Crystal put her head back on her seat and closed her eyes, still in awe of the "moxie," as Crystal's father would say, of this little girl who had gone through so much in such a short period.

Wini possessed a unique inner strength. Crystal knew that Wini's resilience and determination were her greatest assets. With this thought in mind, Crystal drifted off into a peaceful slumber, confident that Wini would always overcome any challenges that came her way.

Crystal was jolted awake by the train's screeching brakes. She felt she had only slept for moments, but it had been more than an hour. Shaking the sleepy cobwebs from her head, she looked out the window. A light blanket of snow covered the ground and the surrounding hills, and the sky was the color of the bluest morning glory. Crystal knew it would be chilly, but she couldn't help but worry if her wool coat was warm enough, especially when she saw everyone on the platform bundled up in thick down coats. The winter sunshine could not disguise the grip of icy cold Maine, and she thought she should have prepared better.

Too late now, she thought as she roused Wini from her nap. "Come, sweetie, we're here."

"LJ," Wini murmured as she rubbed her eyes.

"LJ's right here," Crystal reassured her, tucking the toy into Wini's backpack.

"That was fast," Wini said, turning her head to look out of the window. She began waving frantically, and Crystal saw Duncan, Charlotte, and Lovey on the platform waving back.

Crystal and Wini picked up their duffles, and Wini gave LJ an assuring pat on her head and then slipped her backpack over her shoulders. They walked out of the warm and drowsy air of the train and into the bracing cold of the Maine February sunshine for a long-awaited return to Beach Rose Path.

CHAPTER 35

ENORMOUS CHARACTER

Crystal, Duncan, and Charlotte settled into the welcoming warmth of Charlotte's bungalow. Charlotte brewed a fresh pot of coffee and eagerly opened a box of Take the Cake cookies.

"Lovey, I'd like you to meet LJ. She's just like you, but she lives with me." Wini and Lovey were in the loft, and her adorable introduction of LJ to Lovey made them all smile.

"Charlotte, thank you so much for letting Wini stay here. I didn't really have time to see it at Christmas, but your shop is beautiful," Crystal said after her little tour of the shop.

"Thank you," Charlotte said, pouring the dark aromatic French roast coffee into Crystal's cup.

"Charlotte managed a women's golf pro shop for years. A very successful one, I might add," Duncan chimed in.

Charlotte smiled at Duncan's sweet compliment. He had mentioned on several occasions that her knack for retail merchandising fascinated him, and how she made it seem so effortless.

"And she's done wonders up here in Lobster Claw. She's helping me get my ferry business up and running for this upcoming season, too. Might spread out into a little sightseeing venture. Charlotte sees endless possibilities, and I trust her business judgement implicitly."

Charlotte caught Duncan's flirtatious and loving wink, and felt a hot blush rise into her cheeks. Hoping Crystal wouldn't notice, she quickly got up and went to the kitchen for more napkins, allowing herself a few moments for the flush she felt on her skin to diminish. She knew Duncan would always have this power over her, as her love for him blossomed with his sweet words of endearment.

They chatted for a while longer, with Crystal providing more details on her job as a flight attendant, and what she would do for the next few days in Albany.

"What an exciting career you've had," Charlotte remarked as she cleared the coffee cups and cookie dishes.

"It certainly was," Crystal sighed, leaning back into the couch. "But in all honesty, I don't miss it. Well, sometimes I do, but I have come to a point where I much prefer my feet on the ground instead of in the air. I still like to keep myself involved and up to date on things, which is why I'm substituting for this training class. It will provide a great bonus, too, and it's not too far away. I can't thank you enough for having Wini for these next few days. She's been so excited, it's all she's talked about."

"Well, her vacation calendar is fully booked," Duncan said, describing what he and Charlotte had planned for the week.

"It seems quiet up there," Crystal said, nodding toward the loft. "Would you mind if I went up to check on Wini, Charlotte?"

"Of course not. I was thinking of doing the same thing. Lovey probably needs to go outside, anyway."

"Crystal, just let me know when you're ready to head to the B&B. I am at your service," Duncan said, putting on his jacket. "I'm going to head down to the boat for a while. Just text when you're ready." He gave Charlotte a peck on her cheek and was out the door.

"Before we go upstairs, may I have a word?" Crystal asked, laying a gentle hand on Charlotte's arm.

"Of course." They headed back to the couch.

"I just want to thank you again for having Wini stay here. Like I said, it's all she's been talking about—helping you in the store and walking Lovey. It's obvious you and Duncan have spent a lot of time planning for this week, and I know it's a lot to have a child come suddenly into your life. I'm sure this has all been especially surprising for you."

Charlotte sat next to Crystal. She could see the concern in Crystal's face—her eyes were narrowed slightly and her mouth was a straight line. She wanted to assure her that as much as she was surprised by Wini's existence, she welcomed her. "Duncan and I have both been through some pretty rough times in our past relationships. We're heading into our mid-fifties, and I think when you get older, you know if someone is a good person or not and is worth your time pursuing. I knew Duncan was from the moment I met him, and then when I met his sister, and learned his own history. I knew he was the man I wanted to be with. We have most certainly made plans for our future, but we are both thrilled that you and Wini are now part of those plans."

Crystal nodded toward Charlotte's left hand. "I don't recall seeing that ring when I was here in December. And it's so beautiful, believe me, I would have noticed it, even though I was in terrible pain. Obviously, those plans you just mentioned include marriage?"

Charlotte instinctively looked down at her left hand, the beach rose sapphire and diamond ring sparkling in the pale rays of the winter sunshine that shone through the windows.

"It does. But we don't know when. We're just enjoying our engagement right now."

"I'm happy for you, Charlotte. After all my years of flying, I consider myself to be an excellent judge of character. As soon as I learned Duncan was Wini's father, I immersed myself in researching everything about him, which, professionally speaking, was very easy to do. I researched his architectural firm, and all the awards he accumulated over the years, and even some of his love life. All those Best of Boston awards come with a price of losing privacy, I suppose. I got the feeling, just from what I could find over the last several years, that he was a bit of a Lothario, and one that Isobel fell victim to. I suspect a lot of successful men can be like that. I wasn't sure what I was getting Wini and myself into when I first met you both at The Ski Patrol, but I promised to honor Isobel's wish. I got the sense that the two of you had been together for longer, and I couldn't understand why you were not married. I could see and, more importantly, feel the genuine kindness you each showed toward Wini. I knew it wouldn't be easy, especially for me, but it was my duty to Isobel to make sure Wini got to know her father. I have struggled with my feelings about this, Charlotte, which I won't delve into here, but I am past that now, and I truly see this has been a blessing in disguise."

Tears trickled down Charlotte's cheeks. She sniffled and wiped her face with the sleeve of her sweater. She did not try to conceal her feelings, and she unabashedly let the tears flow, touched by Crystal's heartfelt words.

"I promise you," Charlotte said, taking Crystal's hands into her own, "that we will always be here for Wini. And you. Duncan feels a tremendous responsibility toward the people in his life, whether they are family or friends. It doesn't matter. When he found out about Wini, he was determined to set things right. He planned on letting Wini decide whether or not she wanted to see him again. I cannot tell you how thrilled he was when you were here for the Christmas parade. It was almost as if they had known each other since Wini was born. They clicked so quickly, and their resemblance to each other is still quite uncanny to me. Somehow, I believe they were destined to find each other. I also believe Isobel knew Duncan was a man of enormous character and that, perhaps when Wini was older, she would have found Duncan to let him know about his daughter. I am so sorry about Isobel but I want you to know that we will care for Wini whenever she is here. We love her."

"Now it's my turn to cry," Crystal said, embracing Charlotte tightly. They remained silent, each giving the other a few moments to shed their emotional tears.

"Now," Crystal said, easing back and wiping her tears with her sweater sleeve, "let's go see what those two are up to."

The light of day had considerably lengthened since the winter solstice, which now seemed so long ago. As the twilight sky turned dusky blue, the bungalow's white walls reflected the pink and lavender of the sunset. The ever-present blinking light of Sea Star Lighthouse flashed, and its brightness would increase with the darkening of the sky. A serene hush had enveloped Beach Rose Path as Crystal and Charlotte quietly tiptoed up the steps to the loft.

"I am not surprised at all," whispered Crystal as she and Charlotte discovered Wini had fallen fast asleep on Charlotte's bed, wrapped within the new comforter. Lovey was by her side, fully awake, and her tail gently thumped.

Charlotte kissed Lovey's head. "Good girl," she whispered, knowing that Lovey would not leave Wini's side.

Charlotte walked over to the table near the window and switched on the fairy lights, which cast a pretty and magical glow throughout the loft.

"She's exhausted," Crystal said, putting her hand on Charlotte's arm. "Let's just let her sleep for a little while longer."

Charlotte smiled and the two women made their way back downstairs. They finished up the cookies and continued to chat about their previous lives when both Crystal and Charlotte never knew Beach Rose Path existed.

CHAPTER 36

LOUNGE LIZARD

"Be on your best behavior, young lady," Crystal said as she waited to board the train to Boston's Logan International Airport, from where she would fly to Albany for the remainder of the week. Crystal planned to head back directly to Newport after her trip, and Charlotte and Duncan would drive Wini home, which worked out well, as Duncan had planned to stop into Grayson Dane Kirk on their way back.

Crystal knelt and hugged Wini, who kissed her grandaunt on the cheek.

"Don't worry, I will," she whispered, kissing Crystal again. "I'll miss you."

"I'll miss you, too. We'll FaceTime every day, okay?"

"We will," Wini replied, nodding as she smiled up at her grandaunt.

The train's last call announcement was made, and Crystal grabbed her duffle bag.

"Thank you so much for everything," she said, hugging Duncan and Charlotte in gratitude.

"Don't worry about a thing," Duncan said, his hand resting on Wini's shoulder.

"I won't." Crystal turned to board the train. She spun around, blew them all a kiss, which Wini caught with her hands, and waved goodbye. The chug of the train was loud, and the acrid diesel fumes were strong, but Wini, Duncan, and Charlotte remained on the platform until the train was out of sight and on its way to Boston.

"I think she'll have a good time," Wini said, as she took hold of Duncan's extended hand. Wini looked up at Charlotte and offered her hand, a gesture that touched Charlotte, and she took her hand in hers.

"I like your ring," Wini said, and Charlotte could feel Wini's fingers touch it.

"Thank you. I like it too." Charlotte smiled, and the three of them walked back to Duncan's truck.

"Ready for some Lobster Claw adventures, Wini?" Duncan asked as he securely belted her into the center of the back passenger seat in the truck.

"Ready!" she said, extending both arms in the air in excitement.

Duncan and Charlotte drove off into a week in which a child would be at the center of their focus, something that would be very new to them, but they also knew they were up for this exciting challenge.

The rest of the day flew by, with Charlotte and Wini returning to the bungalow, and Duncan heading to the dock for his daily check on Callum's Pride. They expected Tatiana to arrive later and planned to have dinner at Elsie's Everything before calling it an early night before their trip to Snow Cap Mountain for a day of snowboarding and skating.

They took seats at the counter of the Everything. "Like father, like daughter, huh?" Charlotte laughed as Duncan ordered his favorite double cheeseburger with all the fixings and fries, while Wini had the same. They both ordered root beers, while Charlotte stuck with her favorite: meatloaf, mashed potatoes, and Diet Coke. After desserts of hot fudge sundaes, they started for home.

"That was the best cheeseburger I have ever eaten," Wini said, and a few moments later she was fast asleep in the backseat of Duncan's truck.

When they arrived at Charlotte's, Duncan tenderly unbuckled Wini's seat belt, carefully lifted her from the truck, and carried her up to the loft. He placed his soundly sleeping child on the bed, LJ tucked in right beside her.

"Oh, to be so peaceful," Charlotte whispered as she hugged Duncan close to her. Duncan returned her squeeze, and they slipped down the stairs to the living room.

Charlotte went into the kitchen to make some tea. Duncan sank into the comfy cushions of the couch, which was also an invitation for Lovey to join him, and she snuggled into his lap. Charlotte returned with two mugs of piping hot chamomile tea, its aromatic and flowery fragrance making for a relaxing atmosphere after the incredibly busy day. She placed them on the coffee table, watching the wisps of steam float up from the cups, and the air was filled with the calming scent of the chamomile.

"You're a wonderful dad," Charlotte whispered.

"I hope so," Duncan said, carefully reaching for his mug, mindful as not to spill any accidentally on Lovey, who had moved her head from Duncan's lap to the side of his hip. "Wini makes it easy. She's so good-natured, considering all she's been through. She takes life in stride. We should all be like that."

Charlotte took the seat next to him. "Do you mind if I ask you about Isobel? I'm only curious because I think Wini is such a remarkable girl. Do you think she's anything like Isobel?" She placed her mug on the coffee table.

Duncan turned his attention to Lovey, his hand slowly moving from Lovely's head to her neck, back and forth, back and forth.

"I'm ashamed to admit this, but back in my Boston days, I could be a bit of a lady-killer. Casanova. Lounge lizard."

"Lounge lizard?" Charlotte laughed. "I think you were more of a suave and debonair man about Boston, not a lounge lizard."

Duncan clasped Charlotte's hand and laughed. "Thanks for that," he said, smiling.

"You know what I mean," Duncan sighed. "Eight years ago seems like a lifetime. My life has changed so much. Back then, let's just say I dated. A lot. When I met Isobel, she was a breath of fresh air, always ready for any kind of adventure. She was as fearless as I was with tackling anything—rock climbing, mountain biking, running half marathons. Now that I think about it, it was like we were always competing. She was beautiful, fun, but very intent on being successful, which she was. But so was I, and in the end, especially now, I can see why it never would have worked. But for that one summer, it was fun and exciting, and then she told me she wanted to return to Rhode Island and move her business with her. We parted amicably, again, both of us knowing it would never work between the two of us, but we had a great respect and admiration for each other, too. We wished each other well, and"—Duncan shrugged his shoulders—"that was it. I never heard from her again. Then, of course, I met Melinda and, well, now I'm here. With you."

Charlotte brought Duncan's large, calloused hand to her lips, softly kissed it, and smiled.

"Do you ever wonder that you had to go through all of that—all your skirt chasing," she said with a laugh, "to get to here, with me, Lovey, Lobster Claw? I wonder about it. Did everything that happened to me get me here for a reason? Were we meant to find each other? And now Wini coming into our lives? In such a short time, we met, fell in love, and have a life together, and now a child comes into our lives. How does that even happen?"

"I don't know," Duncan said softly, pulling Charlotte in closer to him. "But we *are* here. I can honestly look back now and say that I am grateful that Melinda was unfaithful to me, and that I had a relationship with Isobel, although fleeting, because she has given me a daughter. And that horrible nor'easter that night in May when I was just about to head back to Boston because I had no electricity, but decided to stop in Elsie's, where my life changed forever." Duncan shook his head. "I don't know what you call it— fate, destiny, or just dumb luck, but whatever the circumstances, painful as they were for both of us, the stars were in alignment and guided us right here, right now, and I would never go back and change a thing. Never. You're the pot of gold at the end of my rainbow. My lucky star. My good luck charm. You're my life."

"Duncan," Charlotte whispered. Even though her eyes were closing, they were drawn to Duncan's lips. She gently ran her thumb over his bottom lip, feeling the ridges of dryness. She slowly pressed her lips to his. The scent of the chamomile tea was enlaced with the woodsy and piney scent of the aftershave on his unshaven face. She felt Duncan's strong hands caress her face as he pulled away from her, smiling that smile, the one that made his eyes dance and crinkle at the edges. The one that brightened his face like a summer sunrise. The one that always captured her heart.

No words were necessary as Charlotte nestled into the loving comfort of Duncan's arms while a light snow danced upon Beach Rose Path.

CHAPTER 37

JOYS OF A SNOWFALL

Tatiana looked out of the bay window of her gallery, watching the snow cover the sidewalks of the Beach Block. The sun had set, and the song of the cardinals, always the last to return to the nest, had ceased. A quiet hush, like the snow, swathed Lobster Claw.

So far, this winter, this was the only type of snow Lobster Claw saw—flurries and dustings that accumulated to only two or three inches. Tatiana recalled one extremely severe winter a few years ago, where snow pummeled the whole of New England every day from the end of January to mid-March. Lobster Claw set a record by recording 120 inches of snow, the most since the early 1900s when snowfall and rainfall were first recorded. But since that winter, Mother Nature had been kind, and the snowfalls hadn't accumulated to more than a few feet, with the exception at Snow Cap Mountain, where the high elevations received all the snow.

They can have it, Tatiana thought. As beautiful as a Lobster Claw snowfall was, Tatiana much preferred the pretty dustings, as it made getting around much easier. She wasn't one to drive in the snow, and she was grateful that there was enough just to make Lobster Claw look like a winter fairy tale.

She shivered at a chill that ran through her, and she turned the thermostat up, instantly sending billows of warm air through the vents. Her attention was then turned to Annabelle's portrait. The portrait was painted in spring, and little Annabelle looked out of a window with bright yellow sunshine streaming through. The trees beyond the window displayed a rich emerald color, resembling glistening jewels, and Annabelle was dressed in a short-sleeved dress. She hoped Annabelle had experienced, at least once in her brief life, the joys of a snowfall—making snow angels, building a snowman, and maybe going for a ride on a little red sled. Next time she and Hamish were together, she would ask him. Even though Hamish told Tatiana so much of his and Hannah's life with Annabelle, it was those little things—like playing in the snow— that Tatiana would forget to ask about. But knowing Hamish, she was sure he pulled that little girl all over the golf course on a sled, and could see her daughter laughing in utter happiness at the delight of newly fallen snow.

My Hamish, Tatiana thought. She missed him terribly, even though they FaceTimed daily; it was not the same as having him physically with her. They had missed so many years together. They wanted nothing more than to be with each other, but there were still loose ends that needed to be tied up. Hamish's family was one. She knew Hamish loved his son, daughter-in-law, and grandson more than anything, and she did not want to cause any friction between father and son.

Tatiana had a great time with Hamish's family in Scotland, and they made her feel nothing but welcome and part of the family. She also knew that Hamish had been honest with Colin about Annabelle. Even though Colin was born years after Annabelle's death, Colin knew he had a sister who died when she was still a toddler. Colin had never once shown any animosity whatsoever toward Tatiana during her visit, but she still couldn't help but think that somewhere inside his heart, he possibly harbored resentment toward her. She considered the situation from an objective standpoint and questioned how she would feel if she were in

Colin's position. She imagined discovering that her own father, during a difficult and troubled phase in his engagement, had a relationship with a woman that led to a pregnancy. How would she feel? Betrayed? Angry? Resentful? Had Colin been putting on an act during her visit?

Hamish had given her his assurance that this was not true; however, they both knew the decisions they were planning for their future would affect everyone—especially Colin.

She walked over to Annabelle's beautiful portrait. "This cannot possibly work without problems, Annabelle," Tatiana said to her daughter. "I just don't know anymore." She jumped as Annabelle's portrait unexpectedly shifted to the left, making the large glass frame tilt.

"Are you trying to tell me something?" she said, laughing. "You're telling me I am a silly fool about your father, or you are telling me to get that hook fixed." She had meant to, as she had noticed the hook had loosened during the busy season, but with her traveling and the holidays, she had forgotten about it. Until now.

Tatiana smiled at the chubby face of the pink-cheeked girl. She adjusted the portrait so that it was straight again and made a mental note to get in touch with Andy to repair it. It was a large and heavy frame, and Tatiana needed to be sure an expert like Andy would take care of it.

"Don't worry." She laughed now that she had righted the frame. "I'll call Andy in the morning," she said, blowing a kiss to her daughter, and feeling somewhat better now that Annabelle had chimed in on her mother's unnecessary doubts.

CHAPTER 38

CHEESEBURGER LASAGNA

Charlotte nursed her second cup of coffee as she watched Wini and Duncan devour their breakfasts at the counter of Elsie's Everything. She just couldn't believe how much they looked and acted alike. They were both left-handed, and each held their fork the same when cutting into the pancakes—they held the fork in a fist and cut their pancakes with their right hands in a saw-like fashion. They loaded their pancakes with nearly half of the bottle of syrup —Duncan pouring syrup on his sausages as well.

Wini had inherited her hair and eye color from her mother, but her other physical characteristics—the deep dimple in her chin, the wide and high forehead, and the twinkling in her eyes when she smiled were all Kirk traits. They both knitted their perfectly arched eyebrows when they were in deep thought, and their mouths formed into straight lines when they were determined or disliked something. They both had the same habit of slightly swaying back and forth instead of standing still.

"I think that's one of the best breakfasts I've ever had," Wini said.

"I think that's the best breakfast I've had, too," Duncan agreed, wiping that determined line of a mouth with a napkin. He finished his coffee just as Elsie propelled herself from behind the flapping black doors that separated the kitchen from the diner area.

"Anything else I can get you?" She smiled as she removed their empty plates from the counter.

"Can we come back for lunch?" Wini asked as she hopped down from the counter stool.

She eagerly slid her arms into her warm puffer coat and tugged her hat securely over her ears. She grabbed her mittens and was ready for a day spent on the docks.

"Duncan, the lunch special of the week is cheeseburger lasagna. Happy to save you and Wini some." This was Elsie's indirect way of letting them know they had better come back for lunch.

"Cheeseburger lasagna? That sounds amazing," Wini said, clapping her mittened hands together. "I've never heard of that before."

Duncan winked at Elsie and left his usual generous tip, full well knowing that he and Wini would be back for lunch. He grabbed some extra napkins and tucked them in his jacket pocket as he liked to keep a reserve in his truck, a habit he picked up from Charlotte, who always seemed to need one.

"You better make us our own lasagna." He laughed as they headed for the door. They stepped out into a beautiful, sunny, wintry day with an inch of powdery snow covering the sidewalks of Sand Dollar Drive. Charlotte experienced her share of pretty snowfalls at Castle Loch, but a snow-covered Northern Maine coastal town was something altogether different—it possessed a unique beauty, with the din of the ocean waves echoing in the morning air. The cawing of the soaring seagulls, diving into the frigid ocean, made this winter wonderland more magical, if that was even possible.

Deeply inhaling the fresh, cold air, Charlotte felt it seep deep into her lungs, cleansing her body and mind, refreshing her, and she was ready to get to work. "You two go on ahead. Lovey and I are going to walk back. It's such a beautiful morning,"

"Are you sure?" Duncan asked, pressing his key fob that emitted a beeping sound, unlocking his truck.

Charlotte kissed his still-warm cheek and caressed it with her gloved hand.

"I'm sure. An invigorating walk after that big breakfast is exactly what I need, and then I'm raring to go. I think it might be busier today because the weather is so beautiful. Tatiana texted earlier there was a lot of foot traffic on the Block, so I better get that coffee brewed." She turned to Wini, who was already inside of the truck, seat belted in the back and ready to go. "You take good care of Duncan Donut, and make sure he doesn't fall into the harbor," Charlotte said with a laugh, leaning inside and giving Wini a big hug. "I'll meet you at Tatiana's later."

"Sounds good," Wini whispered, returning Charlotte's hug. "Are you going to have cheeseburger lasagna with us?" Wini was still leaning out the window as Duncan hopped into the driver's side.

"Hmm, if the store's not too busy, I'll come on down. But if it is busy, I will let you know and you can save me some. How's that?"

"I'll make sure Duncan Donut doesn't eat it all." Wini smiled and settled into the seat.

"You hear that, Duncan Donut?" Charlotte laughed, walking toward the driver's side of the truck. Duncan had rolled the window down and started the ignition.

"No promises," he said, as he leaned out the window and kissed Charlotte.

Charlotte smiled. "I'll let you know how the morning goes," she said.

"And we'll let you know how our morning goes, too. Right, Wini?" Duncan asked, as he put the truck in reverse.

"Right," exclaimed Wini, giving Charlotte a thumbs up, and

she watched them drive down Sand Dollar Drive, taking a left toward the Beach Block and the boat docks.

"We better get a move on, Lovey," Charlotte said, making sure the leash on Lovey's collar was secure, and the two set off on a cold but tranquil walk back to Beach Rose Path.

CHAPTER 39

INDRAKIT

Duncan and Wini spent the better part of the morning on Callum's Pride. He found he loved teaching her proper nautical terminology of the boats such as bow, stern, aft, and starboard. After untying a line from a cleat on the dock, Duncan explained that the boat could be secured either by using a cleat or wooden poles, or pilings.

"This is the important part, Wini, securing the lines. First, wrap the line around this cleat." He pointed to the parts of the cleat that were protruding. "These are the horns of the cleat, and you tie it like you are making the number eight." Duncan wrapped the line in a figure-eight pattern. "You want to do this twice. Now, twist a loop into the line, take the loop, and loop it over the horn and pull it tight." Duncan finished by pulling the secured line as tightly as he could. "This way, your boat is nice and secure. Now I'm going to untie it, and we can try it together."

Wini laid her hands upon his, and she traced his every move. They did this twice, and now it was her turn. She took the line and her hands expertly mimicked Duncan's previously.

"Wini, you're a natural. That's tied perfectly. You'll be captain of your own boat before you know it. Good job."

"Thanks, Duncan Donut. You're a good knot tying teacher. Time for cheeseburger lasagna?" she said with a smile, rubbing her tummy with her hand.

"You picked it up so fast. Let's head back to Elsie's for lunch." Duncan grinned, stood up, and offered a high five. Wini smacked it enthusiastically.

"Auntie Crys says I'm good at in . . ." Wini screwed her face in consternation, unable to think of the word Crystal used.

"Indrakit," she finally said, nodding her head in affirmation. "Auntie Crys says I am good at indrakit stuff like puzzles. She showed me a game she played with string and her hands called cat's cradle. You have to move your hands up and down and make all these indrakit patterns with the string. It was fun. I can show you later."

Duncan smiled at the girl's mispronunciation of intricate. It then occurred to him he did the same *indrakit* thing, except with architecture. "I'd love that, but first cheeseburger lasagna!"

"Yes!" Wini formed her hand into a fist and pulled her elbow down by her side with happiness.

"Let's go." Duncan opened the truck doors, and he and Wini hopped in for a drive down Sand Dollar Drive for their second visit of the day to Elsie's Everything.

CHAPTER 40

OPEN THE DOOR

"I love you, too, Tati. I'll see you tomorrow." Hamish watched his computer screen as Tatiana blew him a kiss and then the screen went blank.

He had just finished his daily FaceTime call with her, and he knew he wasn't himself. How could he be after just coming off a huge argument with Colin about his and Tatiana's relationship? Hamish sat at his desk and looked out the window. It was after seven o'clock and the sky was as black and velvety as a panther. The stars twinkled and dotted the sky, and the green pine branches, covered in a sparkling coat of snow, waved at him from the other side of his window. The hoot of an owl in the distance in the woods behind his home broke the winter's silence.

They'd never had such a heated argument in their lives. Of course, when Colin was growing up, there were the tiffs regarding curfews, driving, and homework, but those little scrapes were just part of parenting a teenager who craved independence. This was different. Hamish shivered at some words that he and Colin had exchanged, and he tried to block them from his mind. What he couldn't block, however, was Colin's angry and red face as he accused his father of never loving his mother, and that he and

Tatiana had probably been in touch this entire time. Hamish couldn't understand Colin's outburst, as he was kind to her when she visited in the fall. Mentioning this, Colin screamed out that it was an act, that he felt he had to be nice, but in reality he wanted nothing more than for her to go back to the States. Colin's words were red hot and fiery with anger, and he may as well have put a dagger into Hamish's heart. Colin then furiously slammed the door so hard it shook the house, and even broke a piece of wood in the door jamb.

Hamish had never seen this side of Colin and it frightened him. Everything Colin accused Hamish of, especially not loving Hannah, was absolutely untrue. Hamish dearly loved Hannah. Did he keep secrets? Yes, he did. He and Hannah were at a very bleak point in their relationship. Hannah's letters from Scotland had become fewer when Hamish came to Castle Loch to work for a year before she joined him. He knew she didn't want to leave her beloved family or Scotland for a new life, but they had made a commitment to each other and were going to be married. That's all that Hamish wanted—for Hannah to be his wife and for her to be happy. But as her letters became less frequent, they also became distant, and the *I miss yous* and *I love yous* were also as infrequent, and Hamish began to experience his own feelings of doubt. It was at this low point in his life and relationship with Hannah that he met Tatiana, and passion trumped prudence. However, full well knowing Hamish was betrothed, Tatiana ended their brief and impassioned encounter, telling him to go back to the life he was destined to live with Hannah. Annabelle's birth brought them back together briefly, but after their daughter's death, life continued on for both Hamish and Tatiana. They each put to bed forever their night together, and the death of their daughter. When Colin was born, life began again for Hannah and Hamish, and theirs was a home once again filled with the laughter and happiness of a child—their own child.

As hard as it was for Hamish, he wanted to be honest with

Colin about everything, feeling now, especially that Colin was happily married and had his own child, that he would understand. Hamish thought his son had, but then what seemed like out of the blue, Colin's attitude drastically changed. Now the bitter storm cloud of Colin's anger hung over him, with Hamish not knowing when it might burst again.

But he was not a man to be intimidated. As much as he loved his son, daughter-in-law, and grandson, Hamish also loved Tatiana to the depths of the world and back. So much had happened to each of them in such a fleeting amount of time so many years ago. They had each reached their seventies and found each other once more. There was no way Hamish would let this chance of a cherished relationship slip through his hands. He prayed Colin would eventually understand, but Colin would not control his father's life.

The loud ping of a text alert rang violently in Hamish's ears. He ignored it and then the pinging became merciless. He angrily sighed and reached for his phone on his desk. *Open the door.* It was from Colin.

Hamish felt his heart speed up so much he could feel it beating, loud and drum-like, in his ears. He became so full of anxiety and nerves thinking that Colin had actually left his home, at Lachlan's bedtime, to continue their fight. With shaking hands, Hamish turned the doorknob and found Colin on his doorstep, his face red and streaked with tears. Hamish reached out his arms, and his son helplessly collapsed into them, sobbing uncontrollably. Hamish tightly held Colin in his arms, his tears mixing with his son's black hair, and no words were necessary for the father and son. All was forgiven.

CHAPTER 41

SHE'S ALL YOURS

Tatiana glanced at her watch. Wini and Duncan would arrive at any minute. She was looking forward to having Wini for a few hours, as she would be a wonderful diversion for her. Tatiana had an unshakable feeling that Hamish wasn't being truthful with her. On their last FaceTime call, she wasn't convinced all was well with Colin and his father's rekindled relationship with her. Hamish didn't make the eye contact the way he always did, and he seemed more fidgety than usual. He was always relaxed in his big leather desk chair, sipping a cup of tea and enjoying his favorite scores as they regaled at their days' events, but hard as he tried to be his happy and jovial self, Tatiana wasn't buying it.

"Oh, it's just cold and damp, sleeting now, and it's just making me tired. That's all, Tati. No worries, okay?" he'd said, trying to convince her nothing was out of the ordinary.

Tatiana tried to shake off the feeling of foreboding. Hamish was in Scotland, and she was in Maine, and she'd promised Wini an afternoon of helping in the gallery. She'd also planned to surprise Wini with a little tea party. She had a pretty set for six with a snowy woodland scene and two deer painted on the cups and the saucers. There was a teapot to match, and if Wini preferred, Tatiana also had hot chocolate, along with chocolate chip cookies from Take the Cake. As a little remembrance for Wini, Tatiana planned to wrap up two cups and saucers for Wini to take back to Newport so she and Crystal could enjoy their own ritual of afternoon tea.

At exactly two thirty, the door to The Blue Hydrangea swung open. Wini and Duncan were right on time.

"Special delivery," Duncan announced as the two of them entered the gallery.

"This is for you," Wini said, beaming. She handed Tatiana a Take the Cake bakery box. "I hope you like it. It's a little coconut cake."

Tatiana took the box, smiling. "That's my absolute favorite. Thank you. Come on in," she said, placing the box on the counter.

Wini took off her mittens, coat, and hat. She looked around the gallery at the framed paintings of lighthouses, beach scenes, and sea creatures such as whales, dolphins, harbor seals, and lobsters.

"This is so pretty, Tatiana," she said, spinning around and taking it all in.

"I'm glad you think so. And I most definitely will need your help in picking out some more paintings to hang on those bare spots."

Wini enthusiastically nodded her head.

"Well, I will let you ladies get to work," Duncan said, bending so that he was eye level with Wini. "Now remember . . ."

"I know," Wini said, smiling. "Be on my best behavior. I will, Duncan Donut."

Duncan wrapped his arms around the little girl. "I had such a good time this morning," he said.

Tatiana's heart filled with affection for the father and daughter as she watched Wini plant a tiny kiss on her father's cheek.

"Me too," Wini said, looking at Duncan with a cheerful smile.

"Tatiana, she's all yours," Duncan said, walking toward her and giving her an affectionate peck of his own. "I'll be at the shop with Charlotte. Something about moving a bookcase." He laughed and zipped up his jacket. "Call if you need anything."

"Oh, don't forget Charlotte's cheeseburger lasagna," Wini called after him.

"Yes," Duncan said, pointing his finger at her. "Thanks for the reminder. She'd be none too happy if that sat in the truck all afternoon."

"Bye, Duncan Donut." Wini waved.

"Bye, Duncan Donut." Tatiana laughed as Duncan rolled his eyes and shook his head in amusement, leaving the two of them in the gallery.

"What would you like me to do?" Wini asked, looking around at the frames on the walls.

"Well, I always start by giving all the paintings a little dusting." Tatiana reached from behind the counter and pulled out a feather duster. A black wooden handle secured plumes of colored feathers, a relic from her museum days. It always did the trick. She handed the duster to Wini.

"Wow. This is pretty. Do you think the feathers are real?"

"Hmm, I'm not sure. But they are pretty and they do the job, especially on the glass. Come on, I'll show you what I do."

Wini followed Tatiana to the large painting of Sea Star Lighthouse. Tiny flecks of dust had become apparent in the winter afternoon sun, and she demonstrated how she lightly dusted away the annoying little specks.

"I think I can do that," Wini said. The next portrait they came to was Annabelle's. "She's pretty." She stared at the picture. "Who is she?"

"My daughter," Tatiana replied.

"Is she all grown up now?" Wini innocently asked, not taking her eyes off the portrait.

"She passed away shortly after this portrait was painted," Tatiana said.

Wini turned and looked up at her. "So, she's with the angels, like my mommy."

The young girl's beautiful sentiment touched Tatiana. "Yes, sweetie, she is."

The shrill ring of Tatiana's phone interrupted the moment. Tatiana handed Wini the duster. "Here, you can start in on dusting, and I'll answer that."

"Okay," Wini said. Wini gently set LJ down on the floor by her side. A wave of affection for the little girl washed over Tatiana. She saw Hamish's name appear on her phone screen. Accepting the request, she whispered, "Hamish, just a moment." She turned and looked at Wini again, watching her sweep the feather duster over the glass frame. Smiling, she returned to her phone call.

"Thanks, Hamish, Wini—" Tatiana jumped at a sudden deafening crash and saw Annabelle's portrait on the floor. It had fallen straight off the hook and was upright against the wall.

"Wini! Are you alright?" Tatiana put the phone on the counter and ran toward Wini, fearful that the large glass frame had fallen on the child and hurt her. Wini stood stock still in front of the frame. She turned toward Tatiana, as big teardrops fell from her eyes.

"I'm so sorry," Wini said, and like a gazelle galloping for its life on the plain, Wini ran out of the gallery.

"Wini!" Tatiana screamed, but the girl had, in what seemed like one quick movement, opened the door and was out of the gallery like lightning. Tatiana ran to the open door, but Wini was nowhere in sight.

"My God," she said, as her own hot tears blinded her. She looked for her phone to call Duncan, and as she grabbed it from the counter, she saw another incoming FaceTime call from Hamish.

"Hamish, I can't talk right now. I have to find Wini," she said, wiping tears from her face.

"My God, Tati," Hamish said. "What's happened?"

"Wini just ran out of the gallery. I need to call Duncan. I'll call you back as soon as we find her." Tatiana disconnected Hamish's call, and with shaking hands, called Duncan.

CHAPTER 42

MY FAULT

Duncan flew down Beach Rose Path in his truck as Charlotte kept her eyes peeled the short distance to the Beach Block. She surveyed the coastline, but there was no sign of Wini. The truck brakes made a loud grinding sound as Duncan abruptly stopped the truck in front of the gallery. They dashed toward the door to find Tatiana standing outside in tears.

"Duncan, I'm so sorry," Tatiana said. She was waiting for them in front of the gallery, shivering in the cold.

"Tatiana, it's not your fault," Duncan said, his eyes scanning the area around them. "Did you see which way she went?"

Tatiana shook her head. "I didn't. It all just happened so fast. I just wanted to be sure she was alright."

"Okay, the one thing we need is to be calm," Charlotte said. "She couldn't possibly have gone far. Tatiana, you go back inside in case she comes back. I'll go to Take the Cake and Harry's. Duncan, you drive up and down the streets. And take Lovey with you."

Even though she was shaking, Charlotte knew she had to maintain her composure. Someone had to. When she lost Landon and Peppercorn, she had gone to pieces, and Hamish was there to pick her up—now it was her turn to be the one who remained calm.

"Let's go, Lovey," Duncan said, attaching the leash to her collar. He quickly kissed Charlotte on her cold cheek. "Get Tatiana inside before she freezes." Giving her the thumbs up he left with Lovey.

Charlotte put her arm around Tatiana and ushered her inside. She then noticed the fallen portrait of Annabelle, and right next to it, LJ. Charlotte knew LJ was always with Wini, and for Wini to leave the little dog behind worried her even more.

"It's all my fault. I knew the hook was loose, but I just got so busy with tourists I forgot to call Andy to fix it." Tatiana sat in one of her well-worn wing chairs, her hands shaking, and Charlotte feared she might go into shock.

"Tatiana," Charlotte began softly, kneeling in front of her. "This was not your fault. Do you understand me? We'll find her. I promise." She saw Tatiana's shawl was draped over her chair. She grabbed it and tightly secured it around Tatiana's still-shaking shoulders. Tatiana gripped Charlotte's hand. She had begun to sob and was unable to speak. "I'm going to get you some tea and then head to Take the Cake and Harry's. If she's not there, I have faith that Duncan and Lovey will find her."

"Never mind the tea." Tatiana pulled the shawl closer around her shoulders. "I'm okay. You go look for her." She wiped her eyes with the shawl and nodded for Charlotte to leave. "Go."

Charlotte bolted to Take the Cake and then to Harry's, but Betsy said she hadn't seen Wini at all and neither had Harry.

Charlotte stood outside of Harry's Surf and Turf. Her eyes began to tear from the cold, and she squinted in earnest, hoping to see some sign of Wini, but she saw none, only a handful of tourists walking up and down the Beach Block as if they hadn't a care in the world. But Charlotte, Duncan, and Tatiana did. Their little Wini was missing. Charlotte's attention turned toward the boat docks. She could see the water with a couple of sailboats bobbing on the waves and thought how silly it would be to be out on a sailboat today. And then it hit her. She quickly texted Duncan, sharing her suspicion about where Wini might be found.

CHAPTER 43

A SECRET

Duncan's mind whirled, almost unable to clearly think straight. The thought of Wini, freezing cold somewhere, panicked him and for a brief moment, his vision blurred with anxiety. He shook it off, and with Lovey at his heels he found his feet carrying him from the Beach Block to the snow-covered dock in front of Callum's Pride. Whether it was instinct, intuition, or a lucky hunch, his feet led him to his boat—the boat where he had spent the morning with his daughter. The boat on which he taught her its anatomy and how to tie a line to a cleat. The boat where Wini seemed happy.

Lovey barked and pulled Duncan closer to the boat.

"I think we've found her," Duncan said, his hand petting Lovey's head. He took off her leash and followed Lovey onboard. Lovey went directly to the cockpit and nosed a blue tarp that was draped over the driver's seat. Duncan quickly pulled out his phone, saw Charlotte's message and texted back, *We've found her. Be back soon.*

Duncan heard sniffling coming from beneath the tarp as it slowly moved, and Wini emerged, wrapped her arms around Lovey, and buried her face in the dog's thick and soft neck.

Duncan stepped closer to the two and sat on the bench opposite the driver's seat. It was unusual to see Wini so distraught; she was always upbeat. Unflappable. Duncan looked at Wini, her face still buried in Lovey's fur. Lovey did not make a move.

Duncan crouched his head and shoulders toward the blue tarp. "You okay under there?" he asked tenderly. He was going to let Wini decide on the next move.

Wini pulled her face from Lovey's neck. Lovey laid down next to her, gently laying her head in Wini's lap.

"Wini," Duncan softly said, coming closer to her, kneeling beside her. Duncan reached to find the pocket inside of his bomber jacket, remembering the napkins he grabbed from Elsie's earlier. He unfolded one and wiped Wini's wet and sad face with it.

Duncan couldn't take his eyes from his daughter, still whimpering, with tears flowing from her eyes. He felt so incredibly sad for her, but he could not find words of comfort. He wanted to, but he, at this moment, felt as scared as she was.

"I'm sorry," Wini said, her voice hushed and barely audible.

"There's nothing to be sorry for, Wini. Accidents happen," Duncan said as emphatically as he could.

"I didn't mean to break the picture of Tatiana's daughter." Through her now heaving sobs, Wini could barely get the words out as tears streamed down her face. "I didn't mean it. Tatiana said that she had died. Like my mommy . . . I want my mommy." Wini's petite frame convulsed with heart-wrenching sobs, piercing the air with anguished cries that no innocent child should ever have to endure. Her thin shoulders shook and trembled, and her cries were like that of a wounded animal.

Duncan picked up his crying child and carried her over to the bench. He unzipped his bomber jacket, took it off and placed it around her writhing body and held her in his lap.

"It's okay," Duncan whispered to the distraught child. "It's okay. Let it out. You've been brave for a long time. It's okay." Wini shook with sobs, as tears that were undoubtedly held back for so long poured from her eyes. Tears of sadness, tears of anger, tears of heartache. Tears for the death of her mother, a mother who was tremendously loved and monumentally missed.

Time stood still as Duncan held his child and let her cry until there were no more tears left. She eventually quieted down and fell asleep in his arms. But he made no move to get up because Wini needed this—the comfort of a parent. She needed him, her father. He would sit in the cold for as long as it took until Wini was ready to leave.

The sun set and the beacon of Sea Star Lighthouse became brighter, shining her ever-present light over Lobster Claw Harbor. The stars glinted in the inky sky, and although it was cold, the night was clear and cloudless as a white sliver of moon hung in the winter sky. Duncan felt the rocking of the ocean and remembered what Charlotte had said the night he proposed—that it was calming and put Wini to sleep, just as it had now. The distress of crying had ceased, and the calm rocking of the ocean was peaceful.

"Duncan Donut?" Wini had opened her eyes and was looking up into her father's face.

Duncan smiled. "Decided to wake up, did you?" Wini sat up in Duncan's jacket. She blinked her eyes, not knowing where she was, and then she realized it when she saw Lovey lying at Duncan's feet.

"We're still on the boat?" she asked, repositioning herself in Duncan's lap.

"We are. I didn't want to wake you." Duncan wanted nothing more than to comfort Wini. He wasn't sure how he was going to do this, but he was determined to try.

"First, I want to let you know nothing broke. The painting just slipped from the hook. Even if it did break, it is fixable. Most things are."

"I know," Wini said, reaching down to pet Lovey, who lovingly kissed her hand.

"Not everything can be fixed," she said, looking up into

Duncan's eyes. "My mommy couldn't be. Tatiana's daughter couldn't be. I know that Mommy is with the angels, but I still miss her so much. She told me never to be sad, and most times I'm not because I know she's happy. But today I really missed her." Wini sighed deeply.

"Why did you miss her so much today?" Duncan asked.

Wini shrugged her shoulders. "I got so scared when the painting fell off the wall. And when I was scared, Mommy would always be there. But she wasn't. And Aunt Crys wasn't there either. I didn't know what to do, and I ran. But I probably shouldn't have."

Duncan shifted on the bench and pulled his jacket tighter around Wini, as a cold breeze had blown in off the water.

"It's okay to be scared," Duncan began, still not knowing what he was going to say. He kissed the top of her head, and suddenly, the words came easily. "But you're never alone, Wini. Never. You have me, Aunt Crys, Charlotte, Tatiana, Lovey—"

"And LJ," Wini interrupted. "I was so scared that I left her at Tatiana's. I hope she's not scared."

"She's not scared at all because she's with Charlotte and Tatiana. See? No one is ever alone," Duncan comfortingly replied.

Wini smiled at Duncan's reassuring words. He continued, "I'm going to tell you a secret. I was alone once. Not too long ago. So I came back here. I came back home. And when I did, my sister was here waiting for me, and then I met Charlotte, and all these other wonderful people, and no matter what happened, I knew I would never be alone again. And neither will you."

"Were you scared, like me?" Wini asked.

Duncan looked into the face that was so much like his. Like his mother's. Maybe because Wini was a child and had such an innocence to her, he felt he could be honest and open, and that's how he answered her simple question.

"I was. I was very scared and very sad. And that's why I came home."

Duncan could feel Wini's arms entwine around his neck as she placed a tiny peck on his cheek.

"And now you found me." She smiled her pretty smile that melted Duncan's heart.

"I did find you. And I'm never going to let you go," he said, hugging her tightly. She giggled, which caused him to laugh as well.

"Can we go back to Tatiana's now? I miss LJ."

He gently removed Wini from his lap, and they stood on the bow of the boat. Duncan reached his hand down to Wini, who put her small hand in his, giving his hand a strong squeeze. Duncan smiled down on his daughter as the three made their way off the boat and onto the dock. Duncan then felt a shift—it was ever so slight, but this shift pushed him from one realm into another; from the realm of simply being a man into the realm of being a father.

CHAPTER 44

An Honor

"Tati, you scared the living daylights out of me," Hamish said.

Tatiana had brought her laptop down to the gallery and she and Charlotte updated Hamish on what had happened with Annabelle's portrait and with Wini.

"I am so sorry to have hung up on you, but she darted out of here so quickly. It was the loud crash, that stricken look on that poor child's face, and before I knew it, she had vanished." Tatiana turned toward Charlotte. "She's faster than Lovey."

Charlotte wrapped a comforting arm around Tatiana's still-trembling shoulders and hugged her close. "She's safe, Tatiana," Charlotte said. "I should have realized she probably ran to the boat, but when something like that happens, all clarity is wiped from your mind." Charlotte caught Hamish's wink and gentle nodding smile, full well knowing she was not only referring to Wini's incident, but to Landon and Peppercorn.

"Well, I'll let you go now and check in with you later." Hamish blew his two favorite ladies a kiss goodbye.

"Any hot chocolate left?" Duncan asked as he and Wini walked in the door.

"Wini!" Tatiana ran to the little girl and engulfed her in an enormous hug.

Wini returned the embrace and whispered, "I'm sorry," into Tatiana's ear.

Tatiana slowly pulled away and looked at Wini as tears formed in the girl's eyes. "Now, no tears. You did nothing wrong. It was all my fault. I knew the hook was loose and I should have fixed it, but I didn't. Nothing broke, and even if it had, it's an easy fix."

"That's what Duncan Donut said," Wini wiped her eyes, and that was the end of any tears.

"Someone's been waiting for you." Charlotte walked over to Wini and handed her LJ. "She's missed you."

"Thank you," Duncan murmured, putting his arm around Charlotte. It was time for the misunderstandings and tensions of the day to be put behind them.

Wini grasped LJ from Charlotte and hugged her tightly, kissing her constant companion. Lovey sidled up next to her and ferociously licked Wini's hands. All was well again.

"And to answer your question, Duncan, there is plenty of hot chocolate. Let me go upstairs and make my special cocoa on the stove. I'll be down shortly," Tatiana said as she headed up her staircase.

"I'll come help you," Charlotte said, giving Wini a tender kiss on top of her strawberry blonde head. She then lovingly touched Duncan's shoulder, and his hand went over hers.

"Take your coat off, Wini," Duncan said, doing the same. "There's something that I want to talk to you about."

Wini did as Duncan asked and handed her coat to him. She snuggled LJ into the wing chair right by her side and looked at Duncan as he pulled up a chair beside her.

"Did I do something wrong again?" she quietly asked.

Duncan shook his head vigorously. "No, sweetie, not at all. Everything couldn't be more right. I just had a question, that's all."

Wini's smile reappeared instantly. "Okay."

"You know, I love that you call me Duncan Donut, right?"

"I know." Wini laughed. "I'm glad."

Duncan shifted in his wing chair, trying to find the right way to ask Wini what he had been thinking about since their morning together on the boat, and Wini's running away had reinforced it all the more. "Well, I was wondering if we could change that a little?"

Wini tilted her head in question. "How?"

Duncan rose and bent down in front of Wini. "I was thinking of something more like Duncan Daddy?"

"Really?" Wini threw her arms around Duncan's neck, hugging him tightly. "I like that even better than Duncan Donut. Duncan Daddy." She looked into her father's eyes, eyes that were now veiled in tears. "Can LJ call you that, too?" Wini asked, holding her friend up to Duncan for his response. Duncan softly kissed the stuffed animal.

"I would consider it an honor," he said as the two shared a heartfelt embrace as father and daughter.

CHAPTER 45

MIRACLES HAPPEN AND LIVES ARE RESTORED

The winter snow that blanketed Lobster Claw had melted. There had been no big snowstorms all winter, but it did snow regularly from the very end of February until mid-March, leaving several inches here and there on the sidewalks of Lobster Claw. Charlotte spent the remainder of winter ordering new merchandise for The Shop at Beach Rose Path. She and Tatiana were planning a baby shower for Ivy, and there was one more event in the works: a wedding.

Duncan and Charlotte had agreed on a wedding date—exactly one year from the day they first met. Wini was beyond thrilled when Charlotte asked her to be the flower girl, and the two spent hours on FaceTime talking about the wedding.

Charlotte had asked Hamish to walk her down the aisle.

"It would be my honor," he had said, tears in his own eyes.

Now, early April, Charlotte stood outside with Lovey as a cool morning breeze blew in the fresh scents of spring. The pretty pastel petals of crocuses poked their heads from the thawing ground in her backyard. She loved the greens at Castle Loch, where it seemed like thousands bloomed every March and April, and she was happy to welcome them back in her own yard.

Now, not only was she approaching her one-year anniversary of moving to Maine, but her wedding day, one of life's milestones. She had completely blocked the thought of ever being a bride from her mind since Landon's death. But life had other plans; plans that brought Charlotte from one life to another on Beach Rose Path.

As she watched the waves break on the sand and the seagulls soar through the morning breeze, she knew that all her heartbreak of the past was worth it since it brought her here—to a place where she had never been happier. Her life was now filled with light and with love.

Charlotte watched Lovey, the little pup who might've died if not for Charlotte, frolic and twirl among the crocuses, and she was sure Lovey could smell spring in the air, too.

And then there was Wini.

Charlotte was past her childbearing years, and she'd poured all of her maternal love into the precious little puppy that was born in her basement. But now there was an actual child she had grown to love.

Although Wini had a mother, and now a grandaunt who was her mother figure, Charlotte hoped that she and Wini's relationship would develop into a special friendship—somewhere between a best friend and an older sister. She realized she felt like a mom when Wini was in Lobster Claw, giving her a glimpse of what it might be like to have a child. The day Wini ran away terrified Charlotte, triggering her somewhat dormant post-traumatic feelings about Landon and Peppercorn, as an almost irrational fear gripped her thinking that like them, Wini had disappeared forever. Of course, all her fears were allayed, but the fact that Wini's disappearance brought them to the surface made Charlotte realize that she had developed a love for this child.

The cawing of the seagulls grew louder, and their cries were now as familiar as the engines of the golf carts every morning on the greens of Castle Loch. She looked up into a robin's-egg-blue sky where foamy billows of white clouds leisurely floated. She watched a few brave souls walk on the beach as icy waves lapped at their feet. She gave them a friendly wave, which they returned and then went back to dodging the lolling waves.

She glanced down at the wooden dock and saw Tatiana waving at her.

Miracles happen and lives are restored. Hamish's mantra echoed in her head, a source of solace following the loss of her boys. Charlotte was undeniably a reflection of that adage.

Her thoughts were interrupted by the buzzing from her phone. If a person's heart could smile, she would swear she could feel hers burst into one now as she saw Duncan's name on her phone screen.

"Good morning," she said, happy that his voice was the first she heard this morning.

"Good morning to you, too," Duncan replied. "I'm ready whenever you are."

Duncan was taking Tatiana and Charlotte on Callum's Pride to Camden to pick up the dresses at a bridal shop.

"Half an hour?" Charlotte said, as she headed back into her shop.

"Perfect. See you soon. Love you."

"Me too." Charlotte smiled as Hamish's words about miracles hung in her ears. "C'mon, Lovey," Charlotte called. "Breakfast and then a boat ride."

Lovey looked at Charlotte and happily trotted inside at hearing her favorite words.

"Miracles happen and lives are restored," she whispered to Lovey, as this rang true for her dog as well. And now the miracle of picking up her wedding dress was about to occur, and her new life as a married woman was about to begin.

CHAPTER 46

MY FAIRY GODMOTHER

"I have no words, Charlotte. Except beautiful. Stunning. Enchanting."

"Tatiana, stop or you're going to make me cry," Charlotte said.

It was now the week before the wedding, and she tried on her dress one last time before the ceremony. Since getting it back from the seamstress in the bridal shop, she had put it on daily, each time shaking her head at the vision that stood before her in the mirror—herself in a wedding dress. It was an A-line ivory tea-length dress with a tulle skirt. The dress had delicate embroidered lace covering her shoulders, even though it was sleeveless. A pretty pattern of leaves was embroidered at the neckline as a sheer muslin material separated the neckline from the bodice. Appliqués and beading of the same leaf pattern adorned the bodice, extending down to the waist, and the sheer tulle of the skirt started from Charlotte's waist, flowing down to just below her knees. The dress fit like a dream.

"A vision, Charlotte. You are an absolute vision." Tatiana put a motherly arm around her shoulder. "And no tears. You look beautiful."

Charlotte stood in front of the mirror, captivated by her own reflection. A beam of sunlight poured in through the windows, casting an ethereal glow, and she felt years younger.

The magic of the sunlight made the gray in her hair pearlescent as it softly cascaded upon her shoulders. Her complexion was that of a newly bloomed beach rose, and her light brown eyes reflected the golden rays of the sun. She wanted to show off the delicate and pretty neckline of the dress and decided to wear her hair in a half-up style. Charlotte grabbed an antique hair clip from her dresser and pinned the sides up as loose tendrils fell, framing her face beautifully.

"I'm so glad you'll wear your hair like that," Tatiana said as she grabbed her tote bag from Charlotte's bed. She pulled out a small blue box and handed it to her. "A little wedding gift."

"Tatiana, you shouldn't—"

Tatiana shook her head. "No, I want to. You are the closest thing that I have to a daughter, and this is my wedding gift to you."

"I know you said no tears, but I can't keep that promise," Charlotte said, teardrops falling from her eyes as she wrapped her arms around Tatiana.

"I know," Tatiana whispered. "I'm so happy for you. Now, open the box."

Charlotte took a tissue from the box on her dresser and wiped her tears. She slowly opened the box that Tatiana had given her. Inside sat a pair of sapphire drop earrings. Surrounding the shimmering blue sapphires were clusters of round, brilliantly cut diamonds. The way they twinkled and shimmered in the spring sunlight was pure magic.

"Tatiana," Charlotte gasped, her eyes glued to the beautiful earrings. "I can't. These are just so beautiful—so special." Charlotte's eyes widened as she gazed at Tatiana.

"They're yours. They were my grandmother's, passed down to my mother, and then to me, and now to you. Put them on."

Charlotte had no words. Her hands trembled as she carefully

clasped the earrings into her lobes. A radiant smile spread across her face as she looked at her reflection in the mirror. The sparkling earrings cast a luminous glow around her face, and she had never felt more beautiful.

"Thank you, Tatiana. I'll cherish them forever." Charlotte hugged her friend once again.

"Well," Tatiana said, sniffing back her own tears, "that's something blue. Your dress is something new. How about something old and borrowed?"

Charlotte shook her head. "You got me on that. Two out of three ain't bad, though, right?" She smiled.

"No, you need something old, something new, something borrowed, and something blue." She reached back into her tote and pulled out tissue paper that was wrapped in a perfect square. A pink satin ribbon was tied around it. "This will knock out something old and something borrowed."

Charlotte took the package, the tissue paper crinkling in her hands.

"Tatiana, I—" Charlotte protested.

"This is something borrowed, so it comes back, remember?" she said cogently.

"Right," Charlotte agreed, knowing that she would tell her to keep it. She delicately unwrapped the tissue paper as a faint scent of lavender wafted from within the folds. Charlotte's breath caught as she lifted the beautiful lace veil from the tissue.

"This belonged to the grandmother of a college friend of mine from many years ago. She was visiting Boston, and my friend had invited me to lunch to meet her grandmother. We attended Mass first because her grandmother was very religious, and she was wearing this mantilla. I remarked how beautiful it was. She only said thank you. A few weeks later, when my friend's grandmother returned to France, I received a package in the mail from her—it was this mantilla, and I have treasured it since. It's time for someone to wear it to her wedding."

Charlotte handled the mantilla carefully. The ivory French net was embroidered with rosebuds and vines. It was incredibly soft and very exquisite.

"May I?" Tatiana asked and Charlotte nodded her head. Tatiana took the mantilla and carefully unfolded it. Standing in front of Charlotte, her deft hands arranged the veil on top of Charlotte's hair. She then took her fingers and whisked both sides of the mantilla so it fell to Charlotte's shoulders and just below her neck. The pretty neckline of Charlotte's dress was still clearly visible, and the mantilla only added to the beauty of the dress.

"Oh, Charlotte." Tatiana whispered. Charlotte turned toward the mirror.

The woman staring back at her was exquisite, like a dream. Her hair, the earrings, the mantilla, and the dress looked like they were all designed with only Charlotte in mind.

"You look as if you've just stepped out of the pages of a fairy tale," Tatiana said, admiring her.

Charlotte glanced into the mirror. "And I feel like it. Thanks to you. My fairy godmother."

Tatiana smiled. "Now, let's get this all put away carefully. We don't want any tear stains on anything, now do we?"

"No, we do not," Charlotte agreed, slowly removing the mantilla from her head.

Tatiana took it and hung it on a silk hanger. Charlotte gingerly removed her wedding dress, also handing it to Tatiana, placing it gently on another silk hanger.

"All put away. When do Crystal and Wini arrive? I can't wait to see Wini in her dress."

"They'll be here Thursday afternoon. Crystal is going to take Wini out of school early so they can catch the one o'clock train, and they should be here by seven or so. We'll have Friday for all our bridal try-ons—again—rehearsal on Saturday and then . . ."

"And then the day you become Mrs. Duncan Kirk. Will you be

taking his name? Sometimes I forget people do things differently now," Tatiana said.

Charlotte smiled at her friend. "I've been Charlotte Templeton for over half a century. I think it's time for a change. Charlotte Kirk has a nice ring to it, don't you think?"

"I don't think," Tatiana said, hugging Charlotte. "I know."

CHAPTER 47

THE LAST SUNRISE

Charlotte opened her eyes to a new day—her wedding day.

Knowing she wouldn't be able to go back to sleep, she got up and went to her bedroom window. She could hear the rhythmic breathing of Lovey, asleep at the foot of her bed. It was still dark outside, and the beacon of Sea Star Lighthouse beamed back and forth over Lobster Claw Harbor. A sunny day, with temperatures between the mid- to high-sixties was forecasted. Perfect weather for a spring wedding.

Charlotte laid back on the pillows and reflected on the day before. Tatiana had taken care of all the arrangements at the Our Lady of Good Voyage Chapel, a stone's throw away from Elsie's Everything. It was a small chapel with an ancient cemetery, mostly the resting places of old Lobster Claw mariners. The delicate lilac bushes were in full bloom, filling the gentle breeze with their distinct and exquisite fragrance. While the beach roses remained dormant, the bright daffodils encircling the church would greet the bridal party with their sunny yellow petals, radiating warmth and cheer. Tulips in every color of the rainbow also were in full bloom, and the pretty pink buds of the apple blossom trees were just opening. The churchyard was a garden oasis.

The woodwork of the inside of the chapel had shimmered as the late afternoon sun had shone through the ornamental stained-glass windows. Charlotte had been a semi-regular church goer when she was younger, but the older and busier she became, the more her attendance dwindled. But she knew she wanted to be married in the church, as an honor to her parents. Pastor Samuel McEverett, Elsie's cousin, was non-judgmental and welcomed the fact that Charlotte and Duncan wanted to make their vows in his little chapel. She felt comfortable in the warmhearted, non-denominational chapel, and it felt right.

The rehearsal went off without a hitch, and then it was on to Elsie's for their rehearsal dinner of double cheeseburgers, with Elsie making sure there was plenty of cheeseburger lasagna for Wini.

Even though she had gone through the rehearsal, Charlotte still had a hard time imagining herself walking down the chapel aisle. Hamish would escort her, along with Tatiana, her maid of honor. Now, in a matter of hours, she would experience the dream of her wedding.

Unable to stay in bed, she got up, went to her closet and pulled out the dress. It sparkled in the dawn of this perfect May morning. An electric-like surge of happiness and excitement raced through Charlotte's blood. Her heart quickened with joyful anticipation as the thought of becoming Duncan's wife was now a reality.

"Coffee will help," she said. Lovey stirred, and they made their way together down to the kitchen. Charlotte opened the door to let Lovey out. She loved her bungalow and store, and she and Duncan planned to stay in the bungalow after they married. His family home was old, and that was going to be one of his next projects, to renovate it to his and Charlotte's liking. They hadn't really discussed it too much, but it would be something Duncan would work on in between his freelancing with Alfred and William and his boat business. So, for the time being, they would live on

Beach Rose Path, and for that, Charlotte was grateful. She wasn't ready to leave her cozy home.

The coffee brewed, and she poured herself a cup. She joined Lovey in the backyard, and together they watched the beautiful sunrise colors of pink and lavender as a bright yellow sun rose over the ocean, and she realized this was the last sunrise she would see as Charlotte Templeton.

CHAPTER 48

NOT BAD, OLD MAN

Duncan Kirk's suit days were over. Or so he had thought. When he had sold his Boston condo, having decided to never go back to the life he led in his Seaport home, he donated all of his suits to charity. He made the conscious decision to go back to his roots and live in his bomber jacket, jeans, Timberlands, and cotton shirts, never thinking he'd be sorry to have donated his suits, also never thinking he would get married. But with help from Ivy, they had taken Callum's Pride to Camden the week before the wedding and picked out his outfit.

"That's perfect, Duncan," Ivy had said, smiling proudly at her big brother as he walked out of the dressing room. They had chosen a navy-blue linen-cotton suit, white shirt and black shoes.

"Oh, Duncan, this would be perfect," Ivy said, coming toward him with a pink silk tie in her hands.

"Ivy, pink? I don't think it's my color." He laughed at what he thought was Ivy's absurd suggestion.

"It's the color of beach roses. Trust me, Charlotte will notice and love you even more."

Her hand instinctively flew to her stomach and her smile

brightened. "The baby just gave me a huge kick—which, I think, is directed at you if you don't listen," she warned.

"Well, I better listen. I don't want any trouble from him or her, when they finally get here," he said with a laugh, humoring his sister and putting the shirt on the counter, along with the suit, shoes, and tie.

"These too." She laughed as she put a pair of pink socks and a pink pocket square on top of the shoes. "Oh, and let me get a tie for your best man."

Now, back in his bathroom, he could see that Ivy was absolutely correct. The light pink of the tie matched well with the suit. He adjusted the matching pocket square, looked at his reflection, and liked what he saw—a man, a groom, on the way to his wedding. And he couldn't be happier.

Things happen for a reason, Duncan. Be patient. His father's voice echoed through his head. Duncan's drive and ambition, and his need for success, always made him impatient. While working at Grayson Dane Kirk, he successfully managed multiple design jobs simultaneously, impressing William and Alfred with his ability to handle the workload. This ultimately led to a partnership, as Duncan not only excelled in creating stunning landscape architecture but also attracted prestigious clients who paid generously for his services. But as his ambition caused his professional star to rise, it most definitely plummeted in his personal life with meaningless romances. The one relationship he thought would last, which did not, led him back to Lobster Claw.

Standing in the bathroom where he got ready for football games, pep rallies, and proms, he now stood with a radiant smile and a full heart, as he prepared for the biggest event of his life. Duncan's smile widened as he finally understood that every twist and turn, every good decision and bad one in his life, had been leading him back to Lobster Claw and to Charlotte Templeton.

Duncan's life decisions also led him to another special female —his daughter. She had changed his life so unexpectedly, and he was truly a blessed man. As the wedding approached, they Face-Timed every day, and Duncan was even more determined to make sure Wini always knew he would be there for her. He had known plenty of men who would have shirked their parental responsibilities if they were in his situation, but once Duncan discovered Wini, and no matter what it took, he wanted—he needed—to win her trust. With Charlotte by his side, and with the support of Crystal, he was able to do just that.

Wini was the flower girl in his wedding, which reminded Duncan of the gift he planned to give her.

He hurried into his bedroom, grabbed the small black velvet box, and put it in his inside blazer pocket. He tapped his chest, ensuring it was there, and he was ready to go.

"One last look," he said as he looked back into the mirror, giving himself one more glance. He nodded, liking what he saw. "Not bad, old man." He smiled, leaving his home to head to the church for his wedding.

CHAPTER 49

A TRUE SCOTTISH HIGHLANDER

Hamish looked at himself in Tatiana's full-length mirror. He brought it down to the gallery as Tatiana was getting dressed upstairs. She didn't want him to see her before she was done.

Hamish made sure to keep his plan of wearing his family's kilt a secret from Tatiana, as he didn't want her to see him either. Oddly enough, Hamish hadn't worn the kilt for his wedding to Hannah; they had opted for a more modern approach, and he wore a suit and tie.

Standing in front of the mirror, he had to admit; he liked what he saw. The deep lines on his face were the lines of his life, and he thought, laughing, made him even more distinguished looking. He kept his weight down with all of his walks and golfing, and he could fit right into the kilt, one that his own grandfather, father, and Colin had been married in.

The kilt was of the Falconer clan, a plaid of dark green, blue and black. His blazer was a navy-blue, as was the matching vest, with a simple white shirt. The color combination was beautiful, with the pink tie adding an extra dash of pizzazz. He adjusted his leather sporran at his waist. Additionally, he chose to wear knee socks in navy blue and paired them with black patent leather shoes.

Hamish was quite astounded by his appearance, not seeing the affable former country club manager in his reflection, but a true Scottish Highlander from centuries ago.

"I must admit, I do like it, especially this," he said, straightening his tie.

"Like what?" Tatiana asked as she walked down the stairs.

"This!" Hamish said with a flourish, as he extended his arms so Tatiana could take in his entire Scottish persona.

"My Hamish."

"Tati," Hamish whispered, forgetting about his own handsome appearance. Tatiana was a vision to behold as she floated down the stairs. Her long, lustrous silver hair cascaded down her shoulders, glimmering in the soft glow of the spring sunshine filtering through the windows. The radiant silver dress she wore complemented her hair flawlessly, creating a celestial aura around her. Around her delicate neck was a strand of pale pink freshwater pearls. Pink pearl earrings also shimmered on her earlobes, and a bracelet to match shone on her right wrist. A large silver brooch adorned the side of her waist. The skirt reached her knees, and a silver pair of slingback shoes graced her feet.

"Tati, you look like an angel descending from heaven," Hamish said, mesmerized by the beautiful woman who stood before him. As he took her hands into his, he gazed upon Tatiana's serene face and was transported back to that day when they first met, so many years ago. She was just as captivating and striking now as she was then.

"Well, look at yourself, my Hamish." Tatiana laughed. "You look magnificent, like a modern-day William Wallace. Dashing, intrepid, valorous and swashbuckling," she concluded.

However, Hamish felt none of those things. "Well, I'm not sure what William Wallace would look like in a kilt."

"He'd look just like you," Tatiana murmured, planting a soft feathery kiss on his cheek. "But I think you look better." She laughed with a wink. "Really, Hamish, you look magnificent."

"I don't think we look too bad for a couple who have lived through seven decades," he said, looking at himself once again in the mirror. He then checked his watch. "Still thirty minutes before I need to pick up Char. Why don't I drop you at the chapel now?"

"Perfect," Tatiana said, grabbing her bag. "I have the rings in my bag. I got a text that the flowers are in the church. I am ready."

"Are you?" Hamish asked, once again pulling Tatiana in close to him for a hug. He looked into her beguiling eyes and saw nothing but love.

"I am, my Hamish. I am."

Hamish kissed her tenderly and put his hand out to her. A powerful surge of love washed over him as Tatiana's delicate hand slipped into this. "Let's go to a wedding." He smiled as they headed out to the chapel.

CHAPTER 50

UNEXPECTED SURPRISE

Charlotte took her wedding dress from the silk hanger and slipped it on. There was a delicate ivory zipper deceptively sewn into the seam of the left side of the dress, so she was able to dress without assistance.

That was so brilliant, she thought as she zipped it up to her underarm. She put her hair into the antique clip, took the earrings Tatiana had given her them from the box, and put them on. She tilted her head back and forth, enjoying the sparkle and the twinkle of the sapphires dancing in the sunlight. She slipped her feet into a pair of ivory satin pumps embellished with a sparkling crystal wreath. The shoes were a splurge, but were so worth it as they gloriously shimmered in the morning sun. Charlotte then moved her engagement ring from her left hand to her right. Duncan would place the band of white gold on her ring finger, and she would wear the engagement ring on top of her wedding band for the rest of her life. She held out her right hand, admiring the beautiful ring.

She gazed into the mirror, mesmerized by the reflection of herself in the breathtaking wedding dress. The clean scent of the ocean drifted in through the open windows, the same therapeutic fragrance she remembered from her first day in Maine. A flutter of butterflies flickered in her stomach, knowing that she was about to embark on a lifelong journey with the man who held her heart. There would never be another moment in time like this for the rest of her life, and she was happy that she could enjoy this alone. Most women about to be married had their mothers, sisters, aunts, and bridesmaids scurrying about, making sure everything was perfect. But Charlotte was not like most women. She didn't have the luxury of a bevy of females fawning over her every wedding-day move—she had just herself and her faithful Lovey, who lay on the bed, her watchful eyes following Charlotte. She turned to her dog and hugged her tightly.

"I don't know what I'd do without you," she whispered.

Lovey's new pink pearl-studded collar was fastened around her neck, and she looked just beautiful. Her tail was thumping happily on the bed, and then out of the blue, Lovey jumped and sprinted down the stairs. Charlotte looked out of the window and saw Hamish had just pulled in front of the house. He was driving Tatiana's car, and Lovey obviously recognized the sound of the engine.

Charlotte was expecting him, and she had unlocked the door. She could hear Hamish say to Lovey as he entered the house, "Oh, Lovey, you look absolutely gorgeous."

"Upstairs, Hamish," Charlotte called as she took the mantilla and gently placed it on her head and shoulders. She could hear his heavy footfalls tramping up the stairs and then a loud gasp.

"Char," he said. She heard the emotion in his voice as he choked back tears. "You are an absolute vision of loveliness."

"Don't make me cry, Hamish." Charlotte smiled, but she could feel her own tears trickle down her cheeks.

"No, tears, Char. No tears." Hamish wiped Charlotte's tears away with his thumb. "You are just such a beautiful bride, and I couldn't be happier for you."

"I wouldn't be here, in this house, in this dress, if it weren't for you." Charlotte sniffled and grabbed a tissue from her dresser. She dabbed at her cheeks and felt the tears stop.

Hamish nodded, smiling at Charlotte. "You've had such heartbreak, Char, and if there is anyone in the world deserving of a good man's love, it is you."

"Oh, my gosh, what is wrong with me?" Charlotte said, extending her arms at Hamish. "Talk about a vision. You look spectacular. I didn't know you would wear a kilt. I love it."

"Well, what's a wedding day without a surprise or two?" Hamish said, laughing.

"Or two?" Charlotte asked, surprisingly. "What are you up to, Hamish Falconer?" She laughed, loving this man who had been her steadfast confidant all these years.

"Or three or four," he said with a cheeky grin. "You never know what the day will hold."

"This whole day in itself is a surprise. Who would have thought, me, a bride?"

"Who wouldn't have thought?" he said, holding out his hands for Charlotte's. "Duncan is an extraordinarily lucky man, and I know that you two will be happy for the rest of your lives. It doesn't matter when you find love, just as long as you do."

Charlotte tightly gripped the hands that held her through her most tumultuous times, the hands that guided her from darkness to light.

"And I am so happy that we found it together," she said, her arms wrapping around the man who had been so fatherly to her for so long.

"Now," Hamish said, standing back, offering Charlotte his arm. "Let's get you to the chapel on time. You, too, Lovey. Let's be off." The three set off for the chapel, and toward a new beginning of their shared lives.

CHAPTER 51

AN OFFICIAL FLOWER GIRL

Duncan stood outside of the church, receiving warm hugs of congratulations from guests as they entered for the ceremony. A black SUV pulled up, and the doors opened, and out popped William Grayson and Alfred Dane, with their wives, Cecilia and Hedy. They all warmly and lovingly embraced Duncan, bestowing their good wishes. He watched as they entered the church and then heard the familiar and distinct engine of another vehicle. He turned to see Andy pull up in Ivy's vet van. Duncan shook his head, humored as he wondered if she brought her small menagerie to the wedding.

Andy opened the passenger door, and in true gentleman fashion, helped his wife from the van. Duncan thought she looked beautiful, even more so at being almost nine months pregnant. She was wearing a very simple white dress with sprays of lilacs printed on it, and a pair of lavender ballet shoes to match. She walked toward her brother with her arms extended and hugged him.

"You look beautiful, Ivy," Duncan said. Her face emanated that legendary radiant glow of pregnancy, with a faint pink blush in her cheeks, and her eyes flashed an extra sparkle.

"Well, you clean up pretty well yourself," Ivy said. Duncan

could feel the pride and happiness radiate from her. "Mom and Dad would be proud." She straightened his beach-rose pink tie.

Duncan gently rested his hand on his sister's belly. "Of you, too," he whispered, hugging his sister as tightly as he could.

"Congrats, Duncan!" Andy had parked the van and embraced his brother-in-law. "I'm happy for you."

Duncan gave Andy's hand a firm shake.

"And how are you doing?" Duncan heard Tatiana's soothing voice and then felt her familiar and comforting squeeze on his shoulder. "Tatiana, you look absolutely gorgeous," Duncan said, kissing her cheek. "I was looking for you earlier."

"I was just in the church office making sure everything was in place. Everything looks beautiful, don't you think? Including you. Look how handsome you are, Duncan," Tatiana said, as he felt her loving caress of his shoulder. "I've never seen you out of that bomber jacket and those boots of yours." She nodded her head in approval. "I like it. I like it a lot."

"Well, don't get too used to it. The jacket and boots will be right back on tomorrow." Duncan was silent for a moment. "Do you think Charlotte will approve?" he asked, feeling a flush rise into his cheeks.

"When Charlotte sees you at the altar, she will think she won the husband lottery. And she has." Tatiana gave Duncan a quick kiss. "I'll see you inside." And she was off.

"Duncan Dad!" Duncan turned to see Wini, Crystal, and Chloe coming from the direction of the parking lot. Wini was waving wildly, and her excitement was palpable with each enthusiastic wave. She was wearing a soft pastel pink dress that shimmered with a subtle sparkle on the delicate rose patterned bodice. A rhinestone sash encircled her waist, and the hem hit perfectly at her knees. She wore pink tights and pink ballet slippers to match.

"I've been waiting for you!" Duncan bent down and engulfed his daughter in a bear hug.

"Duncan, you look wonderful." Crystal stood in front of him, and he embraced her as well. "Wini, I'm going inside now with Chloe. Are you all set?"

"Yes, Auntie Crys, all set. Remember how much we practiced this?" Wini smiled that beautiful smile of hers.

"We sure did." Crystal laughed. "Well, next time I see you, you'll be an official flower girl. Love you." Crystal kissed Wini on the cheek, and she and Chloe walked inside of the church.

"You look beautiful, Wini," Duncan said. He put his hand out to her and led her to a bench in the churchyard.

"You do too, Duncan Dad," Wini said, sitting next to him.

"I have something for you." Duncan took the box from his inside breast pocket and handed it to her.

"Wow," Wini whispered as she carefully opened the small rectangular box. Inside sat a silver charm bracelet, with two charms attached—one of a Labrador retriever silhouette and the other a small rose, fashioned after Charlotte's engagement ring.

"I thought you might like to wear this today," Duncan said.

"Can I really?" Wini took the bracelet from the box and held it up under the sun's golden rays. It shimmered in the sunlight.

"It's Lovey and LJ," she breathed, looking at the pretty charms attached. "And a rose, just like Charlotte's ring."

"I wanted you to have something special to remember this day by. I know how much you love Lovey and LJ, and a little bird told me how much you loved Charlotte's ring, too." Duncan watched the blush rise on Wini's face. She had gushed almost non-stop to Crystal about how much she admired Charlotte's ring, and that one day, she hoped she would have one just as sparkly and pretty. "Here, let me put it on you."

Wini extended her right arm, and Duncan fastened the bracelet around her slim wrist. It fit her perfectly. She held out her wrist and jiggled it, watching the charms bounce in the spring light.

"I love it," Wini said, looking up at Duncan. "Now I have something from my mommy and my dad." She touched the locket at her throat. "This was my mom's and now it's mine."

"It's beautiful, just like you," Duncan said, hugging his daughter once again.

"It's time, Duncan," Tatiana said, emerging from the churchyard.

Duncan stood and kissed Wini on her head. "I'll see you inside," he said, winking at his daughter. He then kissed Tatiana on her cheek and walked inside of the church.

Chapter 52

A Red Red Rose

A hush descended upon the chapel as the strains of "My Love Is Like a Red Red Rose" softly played.

"Oh my love is like a red red rose that's newly sprung in June. Oh my love is like a melody that's sweetly played in tune. As fair art thou my bonnie love so deep in love am I and I will love thee still my dear til a the seas gang dry."

From her place in the back of the chapel, Charlotte watched as the guests simultaneously turned to see Wini, expertly holding onto Lovey's leash. Lovey wore a wreath of flowers that gently bobbed about her neck. Wini softly tossed pink rose petals from a small white basket that hung on the wrist of her hand that held Lovey's leash. In Duncan's gleaming eyes, she saw the pride he felt as he watched his daughter walk down the aisle. He winked at Wini and a proud smile formed on his face. He was so impressed with Wini's composure, giving her father a little wave with her free hand as she stepped into the front pew as Lovey obediently followed.

The strains of the song then became louder.

*"Til a' the seas gang dry, my dear, and the rocks melt with the sun;
And I will love you thee still, my dear, while the sands o' life shall
run. And are thee well, my only love, and fare thee well a while. And I
will come again my love, Tho' it were ten thousand mile."*

The guests turned once again. Shafts of sunlight poured through the stained-glass windows of Our Lady of Good Voyage, creating colorful prisms that reflected on the highly polished oak pews and aisle of the church. Hamish and Charlotte began their walk down the petal-strewn aisle, and she felt all eyes were on her and her handsome Scottish escort.

Charlotte's heartbeat pounded in her ears as the soulful and beautiful song played. She arranged the mantilla so that it obscured her face, and she looked at the guests in the church through the lace edges. Although she recognized everyone, they somehow didn't register. For her, at this moment, only two people existed in the church—she and Duncan.

As she approached the altar, her eyes locked with her groom. She had never seen Duncan look more handsome, and she saw his playful and subtle smile, and she knew immediately that nothing but a lifetime of love awaited her. Awaited them.

Hamish loosened his arm from Charlotte's. As Hamish moved behind him, Duncan stepped away from the altar to stand next to Charlotte; Tatiana then walked from the front pew to stand with the bride. Charlotte took a breath, a warm flush rising into her cheeks as Duncan's gaze met hers. She was lost in love, oblivious to everything else except for herself and Duncan.

Pastor McEverett began the service.

"Thank you all for coming today for the marriage service of Charlotte Templeton and Duncan Kirk. Charlotte and Duncan, as you may have already guessed, wanted a Scottish touch to their wedding to pay homage to Duncan's ancestry and to Hamish Falconer, who was instrumental in Charlotte and Duncan's relationship. Duncan and Charlotte have chosen to recite a Celtic wedding vow. Duncan, please take Charlotte's hands, and when you are ready, you may begin."

Charlotte felt his hands tremble as he took hers in his.

He took a deep breath and began. "You are the star of each night. You are the brightness of every morning. You are the story of each guest. You are the report of every land. No evil shall befall you, on hill nor bank, in field or valley, on mountain or in glen. Neither above nor below, neither in sea."

Her racing heart thumped in her chest at the sound of his voice reciting his vows. Overwhelmed by an incredible love for him that coursed through her, it was now her turn to express her love to him.

"Nor on shore, in skies above, nor in the depths. You are the kernel of my heart, you are the face of my sun, you are the harp of my music. You are the crown of my company."

"Beautiful," Pastor McEverett said. "Duncan Kirk, do you take Charlotte Templeton to be your loving wife?"

"I do." Hamish handed Duncan the delicate white gold band. He placed it on Charlotte's finger. "With this ring I thee wed."

"Charlotte Templeton, do you take Duncan Kirk to be your loving husband?"

Charlotte couldn't help but smile. "I do." Tatiana handed Charlotte Duncan's thick white gold band, and she slipped it on his finger. "With this ring I thee wed."

The church echoed with sniffles as attendees were moved by the tender and beautiful ceremony.

"With the power vested in me, I pronounce you husband and wife. Duncan, you may kiss your bride," Pastor McEverett concluded.

Duncan stepped forward, his hands brushing Charlotte's face. She could feel his breath on her face as he delicately pushed aside the mantilla, lovingly caressing her cheeks.

"I will always love you, Charlotte," he whispered.

He leaned in and the scent of his piney and woodsy aftershave filled the air around her. As his lips alighted upon hers, a surge of love sent an electric current through her body, imprinting this tender moment within her mind forever—the moment she became Charlotte Kirk.

Cheers erupted within the church as the bride and groom turned and waved to their guests, who waved back at Mr. and Mrs. Kirk at the altar. Love and happiness overwhelmed Charlotte as Duncan took her hand in the chapel.

"Now it's our turn," he said with that mischievous quirk of a smile that always appeared when he had something up his sleeve.

"Our turn for what?" Charlotte asked with a sly smile of her own.

"To be wedding guests," Duncan said, escorting Charlotte into the first pew next to Wini.

Once again, a hush covered the church like newly fallen snow in winter. The strains of a violin played, and a beautiful and angelic voice began to sing.

"Oh rowan tree, oh rowan tree, thou'll aye be dear to me, entwined thou art wi' many ties of hame and infancy. They leaves were aye the first of spring, they flowers the summer's pride, there was a name such a bonnie tree in all the country side. How fair were though in summer time, with all they clusters white, how rich and gay they autumn dress, wi' berries red and bright. On they fair stem were many names which noun more I see, But they're engraved on my heart, forget they ne'er can be. Oh Rowan Tree."

The singing stopped, and Charlotte, still not understanding what was going on, looked back in the church and saw a beautiful young woman with long chestnut hair holding a microphone in her hand. She looked somewhat familiar, but then Charlotte's attention shifted to a woman who began to walk down the aisle, holding a small bouquet of pink roses. The woman was Tatiana.

Charlotte quickly whipped around and saw the distinguished

Hamish standing at the altar where Duncan stood moments ago. He nodded slowly toward Charlotte, as Charlotte's hands flew to her mouth in surprise. She looked at Duncan, who wrapped his arms around her, and she melted into his strong and loving embrace. As Tatiana approached the center of the aisle, the woman sang again.

"We sat beneath thy spreadin' shade, the baronies round thee ran, they pu'd they bonnie berries red, and necklaces they strang. My mother, oh! I see her still, She smiled our sports to see with Jeannie on her lap, and Jamie on her knee. Oh Rowan Tree. Oh Rowan Tree."

Just as Tatiana was about to join Hamish, Charlotte noticed a young man walk up the side aisle on Hamish's side. Colin. It was then that Charlotte realized the woman singing at the back of the church was Haleigh. Charlotte had never met Haleigh in person but had seen pictures of her in Hamish's office. Was Charlotte the only one who didn't know Tatiana and Hamish were getting married as well?

Duncan loosened his embrace. "Here," he whispered and handed Charlotte a simple gold band. She kissed her husband and left the pew to join Tatiana at the altar.

"A double wedding," Pastor McEverett exclaimed, "will be as lucky as a double rainbow." He then proceeded with the more traditional vows of a wedding ceremony, where Hamish and Tatiana promised to love, honor, and respect each other for as long as they both shall live.

Colin handed his father Tatiana's wedding band, and the father and son embraced. Hamish then held out his hand and slid the gold band onto her finger. Charlotte handed Tatiana Hamish's ring, and she slid the gold band onto his ring finger.

"You may kiss your bride, Hamish," Pastor McEverett said, a smile spreading across his kindly face.

Tatiana and Hamish stepped toward each other, and Charlotte

could see the love they had for each other in their eyes. After all these years, through births, deaths, marriages, and separate lives, now it was their time. It was their turn to live the rest of their own lives as husband and wife.

Their lips met in a loving kiss, and once again, the guests erupted into cheers.

"Charlotte, I'm so sorry. I wanted to tell you, but, well, this one wouldn't let me," Tatiana whispered.

Charlotte was hugging Tatiana as tightly as she could and laughing with happiness.

"I can't believe you all kept it from me," she exclaimed.

"I told you there'd be a surprise or two," Hamish said, hugging Charlotte and then Duncan who was now at the alter.

"That you did," Charlotte said, and now the tears were flowing, and she was not even going to stop them. "I am so happy and so honored that we were married on the same day. You have no idea." Charlotte collapsed into Tatiana's arms.

"Everyone, everyone, I am so sorry," Pastor McEverett began. "With all this happiness, I forgot to formally introduce our newly married couples. Everyone, I am so proud to present to you Mr. and Mrs. Duncan Kirk and Mr. and Mrs. Hamish Falconer!"

Cheers loudly arose once again as Charlotte and Duncan and Tatiana and Hamish made their way down the aisle, soft rose petals being tossed upon them as they made their way out of the church.

CHAPTER 53

HE'S BEAUTIFUL

"Elsie, this is amazing. I never knew this existed," Charlotte said, astounded by the inviting function room tucked away in the back of the diner. Streamers in vibrant colors resembling Lobster Claw sunrises and sunsets decorated the room. Balloons every color of the rainbow floated throughout with messages of "Just Married" and "Congratulations" skimmed the ceiling.

"I only use it for special family occasions. And as this is a very special occasion. Especially since you and Duncan met here, well, I consider you family." Elsie hugged both Duncan and Charlotte. "Now, let the wedding feast begin! Family style!"

A long banquet table, covered in a blue tablecloth, was arranged by Elsie. She and her son loaded the table with the best of Elsie's diner food—meatloaf and mashed potatoes, cheeseburger sliders, individual-sized chicken pot pies, fried chicken, and, of course, cheeseburger lasagna, along with a huge colorful salad and just-baked rolls.

Charlotte piled her plate with the meatloaf and mashed potatoes, and Duncan helped himself to several cheeseburger sliders and a generous portion of cheeseburger lasagna, as did Wini. To add a cozy and charming touch to the reception, Elsie had set up small round tables with foldable chairs. Betsy from Take the Cake wheeled in a table carrying two three-tiered cakes. One cake was decorated with pink buttercream frosting and real pink roses. The team at Take the Cake frosted the other cake with white buttercream frosting and adorned each layer with delicately placed blue hydrangeas.

Charlotte and Tatiana looked at each other in utter surprise. The cakes were truly beautiful as Betsy's cake decorating skills were brilliantly showcased.

The clinking of a knife on a wine glass interrupted the approving oohs and ahhs.

Colin stood with a champagne glass in his hand. "I promise to make this short so we can all dive right into those amazing looking cakes," he said with a laugh, his Scottish accent charming.

Colin held up his glass. "To my father, Hamish Falconer. There is no one in this room who is happier for you than I that you have found love again. May it last forever and beyond." Everyone lifted their glasses and toasted Tatiana and Hamish. Hamish and Colin embraced, and Hamish remained standing, lifting his glass again.

"I may not be as good as my son in his brevity, but I will try. To Charlotte and Duncan. Cheers to a very happy life together." Hamish then directed his gaze solely upon Charlotte. "And Charlotte, Char, a simple Scottish quote from Mary Queen of Scots that suits you perfectly. To be kind to all, to like many and love a few, to be needed and wanted by those we love is certainly the nearest we can come to happiness. To your happiness." Hamish lifted his glass and everyone toasted. Charlotte put her glass down and ran into Hamish's arms, hugging him lovingly. He kissed her cheek and hugged her in return and said, "And now to quote Marie Antoinette—we shall have our cake and eat it too."

Tatiana, Charlotte, and Elsie cut slices of cake, which everyone took enthusiastically. Wini took a piece of each and rolled her eyes in delight at the deliciousness.

"Best cake I ever had!" she declared, as others followed suit to enjoy the cakes.

"Remember when we first had Betsy's cake?" Duncan asked, spooning a piece of the white cake that contained a rose.

"I do," said Charlotte, eating a piece of the flaky cake. It was velvety, moist, and absolutely delectable. "The night of Harry's bonfire at The Blue Hydrangea. I was having a champagne float, and you tried to share my cake with me." She smiled at the sweet memory of that evening last year.

"And now I know better not to," he said, kissing her butter-cream frosted lips.

She delicately licked the creamy frosting from her fingers, enjoying its sugary taste, but her fingertips were sticky, and she did not want to get any on her dress.

"Be right back. Just going to wash the frosting from my hands," Charlotte whispered, kissing her husband once again.

Charlotte walked into the restroom, soaped up her hands, and turned on the water. As she watched the suds flow down the drain, she quickly turned off the faucet, thinking that she heard a voice.

"Hello?" she called. She looked around the restroom, but it was empty. She wiped her hands, thinking that the voice was actually from the party.

"Charlotte?" The voice was coming from the end stall but sounded so far away.

"Ivy? Is that you?" Charlotte asked, heading toward the voice. She laid her hand on the stall's knob, but found it locked.

"Ivy, what's wrong?" Charlotte felt panic rise in her throat.

"The baby's coming," Ivy whispered breathlessly as she unlocked and opened the door. There stood Ivy, her pretty lilac ballet slippers drenched from her broken water. Charlotte saw her grimace as a contraction stabbed her abdomen, causing Ivy to bend over in pain.

"Ivy, I promise, I'll be gone two seconds." Charlotte dashed out of the restroom, scanning the function room for Chloe, who was sitting with William and Alfred and their wives.

"Chloe, I need you in the ladies' room." She grabbed Chloe's arm, practically dragging her to the bathroom. Charlotte then saw Andy.

"It's Ivy," Charlotte whispered. "She's in labor."

"Oh my God," was all Andy could say, following Charlotte and Chloe into the ladies' room.

Charlotte brought Chloe to the end stall, and Chloe lifted Ivy from the toilet seat. Andy took hold of his wife's arms as he and Chloe guided Ivy to lie down on the floor.

"Andy, take off your jacket so we can put it underneath Ivy," demanded Chloe.

Andy whipped off his jacket and put it on the floor. They carefully laid Ivy down upon it.

"Andy, kneel behind Ivy and let her use your lap as a pillow." Chloe checked Ivy and saw the crown of the baby's head. "Coming in fast." She quickly got up and washed her hands as Andy held his wife's head in his lap, whispering words of encouragement.

"Ivy, concentrate on your breathing, okay?" Chloe's voice was commanding but reassuring, as it was obvious this was not her first delivery.

"What can I do?" Charlotte asked, holding onto Ivy's sweaty hand.

"Nothing yet, but I'll let you know. Okay, Ivy, give me one push." Ivy followed Chloe's instructions and did what she was told. The baby's head fully emerged, and Chloe put her hand on the head to support it, making sure it did not touch the floor.

"Keep breathing, Ivy. You're doing great," Chloe said as she guided the baby. The baby's shoulders and the rest of its body soon followed.

Chloe cleaned the baby's nose with her sleeve to expel any extra mucus and amniotic fluid. With the cord still attached, Chloe put the baby onto Ivy's chest. "Congratulations, Ivy," Chloe smiled, "you're a mom to a beautiful baby boy."

The baby's boisterous cries filled the restroom.

"He's beautiful," Andy murmured, gently putting his hand on his son's head.

"Okay, Charlotte, get Elsie to get you all the clean towels she has, and I'm going to call 911. The placenta should deliver itself within the next thirty minutes, so the EMTs should be here by then. Everything is great."

"Charlotte!" Duncan yelled as he saw his wife hastily emerge from the ladies' room.

Upon hearing her husband's voice, Charlotte broke into tears. She had never seen, never mind assisted with the birth of a baby, and the miracle of a new life entering this world, let alone on her wedding day, was emotionally overwhelming. Feeling drained, she fell into Duncan's loving embrace. "Oh, Duncan," she said, hugging him tightly. "You're an uncle!" She felt his lips on hers and then snapped back to reality. "I've got to get towels. Be right back."

Within moments, Charlotte returned with clean towels and helped Chloe wrap the baby and Ivy within them. Charlotte let Duncan in, and he knelt at his sister's side.

"Meet your nephew, Callum," she said through her happy tears as she introduced her son to her brother.

While the guests were celebrating, eating cake, and drinking champagne, they were unaware that not only on this double wedding day, there was also a birthday. The EMTs rushed in, and the next thing the guests saw was Ivy on a stretcher with a baby in her arms. Then, as in the chapel, cheers rose from the guests as the new family was bundled into the ambulance.

"I think I need another glass of champagne," Charlotte said with a laugh, walking back to her table. Duncan topped off their glasses, and they clinked in celebration. They quickly downed the champagne and were ready for another.

"Amazing," Tatiana said, sitting next to Duncan and Charlotte. "Who would have thought?"

"Not me, that's for sure," Hamish said, joining them. Elsie had moved the tables closer to the wall to make room for a dance floor. Kool and the Gang's "Celebration" filled the room as the CD player played and the guests danced.

The two newly married couples watched their friends and family out on the floor, all dancing their hearts out in celebration of the day. Charlotte turned toward Duncan, Hamish, and Tatiana and simply said, "I am the luckiest woman in the world."

"Next to me," Tatiana said, getting up and kissing Charlotte on her wet cheek.

Wini eagerly dashed to the table where the foursome sat.

"Come on, Duncan Dad. Dance!" Wini moved her feet wildly and spun around so that her dress flowed like a fairy princess.

Duncan turned toward them all and laughed. "Let's go," he exclaimed. They celebrated with friends and family on the dance floor, commemorating a wonderful day.

CHAPTER 54

LET'S GO HOME, MRS. KIRK

The gentle roll of the waves washed over Charlotte and Duncan's bare feet. It was after midnight. All guests departed by eleven, but Crystal and Wini left earlier as Wini had fallen asleep in Duncan's lap. Chloe invited everyone to the B&B in the morning for a wedding breakfast before the out-of-town guests had to depart. Wini had been particularly excited about it as Chloe promised her she could help make it. But neither Duncan nor Charlotte could sleep. They walked the beach, hand in hand, with Lovey by their side.

The beacon of Sea Star Lighthouse shone over the beach and the craggy rocks on which it stood. Duncan and Charlotte sat on those rocks, and Lovey curled up beside them, quickly falling asleep.

Duncan put his arm around Charlotte, pulled her in close, and kissed her on top of her head. Charlotte had never felt more loved in her life than she had on this day—her wedding day.

"What a day," Duncan whispered as they watched the gentle waves roll in and out.

Charlotte looked up at him and smiled. "You not only became

a husband, but you're an uncle now, too," she said, pulling his arm tighter around her shoulder.

"And whose husband am I?" he teased, tightly embracing Charlotte.

"You are all mine," she said, leaning her face toward his. She could see the love in his eyes as that quirk of a smile appeared on his lips, and the dimple in his chin deepened. He bent in and kissed her deeply. Charlotte felt the cool sea breeze caressing her skin as the crashing of the waves grew louder, and as Duncan's lips pressed upon hers, the sound fused with his passionate kiss. In that moment, she could feel the intensity of his love, as if the crashing waves were enveloping her, sweeping her away where only their love existed. Charlotte could hear her heart pounding as the scent of the brine on the craggy rocks, along with Duncan's ever powerful piney aftershave, engulfed all of her senses. She was truly lost in love.

As their lips parted, no words were needed. Charlotte nestled deeper into Duncan's warm leather bomber jacket, relishing the touch of its soft, worn, and familiar feel against her cheek.

With a gentle motion, Duncan stood and reached out his hand to his wife. "Let's go home, Mrs. Kirk," he said, intertwining his fingers with hers, and they made their way home to Beach Rose Path.

Rate and Review

We hope you enjoyed *The Rocking of the Ocean* by Barbara Matteson. If you did, we would ask that you please rate and review this title. Every review helps our authors.

Rate and Review: The Rocking of the Ocean

About the Author

Barbara Matteson is the author of The Perfect Mrs. Claus, Beach Rose Path, and The Rocking of the Ocean. The picturesque New England states serve as the setting for her stories, having lived in the area all of her life. She lives outside of Boston with her husband, son, black Labrador Retriever, and leopard gecko. Her job on Boston's scenic waterfront provides great inspiration for her writing.

Other Titles from
5 Prince Publishing

www.5PrinceBooks.com